The Disapproving Duke

"I have observed your behaviour this evening. I am thus unsurprised that after flinging yourself at half the gentleman in the room, you - no doubt drunkenly - fling yourself at yet another victim."

Diana gasped in bewilderment. What could he mean by such an attack? Thoughts and questions raced through her mind: had her conduct been reproachable? Had she made a spectacle of herself?

The Duke continued. "Mores may be different among the younger people of today, but for a married woman to comport yourself as you do is a disgrace. I can only pity your husband and child, that you humiliate yourself and dishonour your family in this fashion." His voice was low and grave yet held the emotion of deep anger.

Despite her shock, Diana began to realise that some hideous error had been made. The Duke clearly mistook her for some other woman. She did not know how this mix up had occurred, nor why he had chosen to berate her in this manner. She was mortified both for herself and for him.

With no further words, the Duke of Eastleigh turned sharply from her and departed.

BY THE SAME AUTHOR:

The Substitute Bride

"There's no need to act the blushing maiden. We both know all too well the circumstances that led to our union."

When Lily secretly takes her cousin's place in an arranged marriage, little does she realise the desire, or the dangers, that await her.

The Marquess of Westford only offered to marry disgraced Elizabeth Cosgrove to save her family's honour. He has no idea that an innocent girl has taken her place.

When the passion he arouses in Lily only confirms his belief that she's a wanton, how can she ever convince him of her virtue?

Teaching His Ward

"Remember only that you must yield, Jemima, to whatever your husband may demand of you. There is no place for maidenly coyness between man and wife."

Jemima is determined to make her debut in society - but her strict guardian, whom she's never met, won't allow it.

But when she runs away to London and falls for a handsome aristocrat, she's in for a big shock.

Having entrusted her education to others, her guardian, Marcus Harlington, Earl Southwell, now desires to play personal tutor... in teaching her some rather more wifely duties.

THE DISAPPROVING DUKE

NOËL CADES

First Printing, 2020

ISBN-13: 978-0-6480874-6-5

This book is dedicated to Linden & Victoria

CHAPTER 1

When a family has suffered genteel poverty for many years, they may be forgiven for being overwhelmed with excitement at the news of an unexpected legacy.

Such was the mood at the breakfast table when Mrs St Clair, a widower, revealed to her daughters the details of her interview with the family solicitors.

"But who is Lord Henry Harrogate?" her eldest daughter, Maria, demanded. "And what has he left us?" Maria had the dark hair and brows of her mother if not the same fineness of feature. She was a handsome girl who tended to haughtiness despite the St Clairs' reduced state.

"He is a very distant cousin, my dear. In truth I barely knew of the connection, but it appears he died unmarried. The solicitor had little information as to his character or circumstances. Except that he owned a flock of rare sheep, and was most concerned for their welfare in the event of his death."

"Sheep! Do not tell us we are to become shepherdesses," exclaimed Henrietta, the second sister and the acknowledged beauty of the family. With light brown hair that curled prettily around her face, and a delicate pink-and-white complexion that the sun had graciously refrained from freckling, she had bitterly regretted the absence of fine gowns and pretty falfals that might have won suitors.

Patiently, Mrs St Clair continued her tale. "No, my dear. He has entrusted this flock to us, indeed, but there is more." She had grown pink, a fact which alarmed her youngest daughter Diana, for Mrs St Clair had a delicate constitution. The doctor had warned that she should avoid strain. "He has also bequeathed us the entirety of his estate."

Maria was scornful. "And what might that be? A leaking farmhouse in the wilds of the Yorkshire moors, no doubt, and more debt than a few bales of wool and mutton will ever settle."

"It is a sum of some eighty thousand pounds."

The mouths of all three daughters fell open in a most unladylike fashion.

"Eighty thousand pounds?!" Henrietta was overcome with a glittering vision of grand houses, balls, fine clothes and fine people. The walls of their small cottage seemed to dissolve about her. Poverty no more! They were rich, rich beyond imagining.

Maria's first thought was the reaction of former friends who had shunned them since their father's death. How the tables might be turned now! The forgotten Misses St Clair, poor mice who eked out a living in a rented hovel, would be the rich Misses St Clair, at the height of society.

Only Diana, though she were overwhelmed by such a sum, felt anxious. A fortune of that magnitude would not come without great change and responsibility, and she feared for her mother's health. Reining in the exuberance and likely excesses of her sisters would be a task in itself. Diana had a little knowledge of financial matters. She was aware that eighty thousand might well be squandered as rapidly as five thousand.

Over the years Diana had helped her mother look after the small investments that remained after the St Clair estate was sold to settle the family's large debts. The late Rainault St Clair came from a noble family, greatly decayed in wealth. Generations of St Clairs, insouciant as to their dwindling fortunes, had sought pleasure with little concern as to how the family's situation might be repaired.

Rainault was the last of these, save for some very distant St Clairs who had moved abroad in the previous century. Handsome, popular, carefree, he had fallen instantly in love with the orphaned Catherine Harborough at a ball. She was a girl of great beauty and excellent nature but without dowry or expectations. Rainault had married her without a second thought as to how he might support her. When he died unexpectedly early, leaving her a widow with three young daughters, the true picture of their debts had become clear. Only a very careful management of what remained had saved them from total penury.

"The solicitors are quite sure there will be no other claimants on the estate?" Diana asked.

"I believe so," Mrs St Clair said. She regarded her youngest daughter. At seventeen, barely out of the schoolroom, no one had given much attention to Diana. But over the years Mrs St Clair had secretly observed her growing into the image of her father: golden haired, noble featured, with the promise of the great beauty of the St Clairs. It was the differences that struck her now. With some pain she reflected how light-hearted and carefree Rainault had been, whereas Diana held the weight of the world on her young shoulders.

"We must take a house in London at once," Maria announced. "In the very best neighbourhood. We may take it furnished, for there is little time to arrange that ourselves."

Henrietta agreed. "It is half way through the season already, but no doubt that will make us even more of a sensation. We must order gowns straight away. I shall engage the most fashionable Parisienne modiste. And a carriage. When does the money come, Mamma?"

Diana saw that her mother was looking strained at these plans. She knew the doctor would strongly advise against any such move. The bad air and bustle of a city would be perilous to Mrs St Clair's health. As young as she was, Diana knew she must be firm with her sisters for her mother's sake.

"These matters typically take months to settle," she informed them. "And I do not think the doctor would advise London at the present time."

Grudgingly, Maria and Henrietta were forced to acknowledge the truth of this. As selfish as both could be, they loved their mother and did not wish to exacerbate her frail condition.

"We might take a house in Bath, then," Maria suggested. Their current residence, in Didmarton, was but fifteen miles from that city.

Diana did not consider her mother fit for Bath but held her tongue for the present.

"At any rate I shall see at once about remedying the shame of our current wardrobe," Henrietta said. "I am sure that we may be given credit, based on our expectations. For I cannot bear these rags a moment longer." Henrietta looked disdainfully at her sprigged muslin, of which the simplicity did more to enhance her prettiness than she realised. Henrietta's ideal of style was very much more lavish and ornate.

While Maria and Henrietta went to devise increasingly grand plans for their re-entry into society, Diana saw no reason to alter her morning routine. After such tumultuous news the familiar would be a balm. On a typical weekday morning this involved reading the previous day's newspaper - kindly provided by a neighbour conscious of the St Clairs' need for small economies - and determining whether any instructions should be sent to the firm who handled their investments.

Mrs St Clair's education had been that considered fit for a girl in her day and ran more to music and needlework than to financial affairs. She had little knowledge of or head for figures. But she had a keen intelligence which her youngest daughter had inherited. Over the years a careful eye on grain and wool prices had halted the decline of their modest capital, and of late had increased it by some small measure. If Diana were occasionally tempted by the sensation of a silver mine, she kept her speculative urges in check. It would not do to squander what little means they had.

"I will write to Jocasta Harcourt," Mrs St Clair said, as Diana pored over the small newsprint. They were lucky indeed to have the privilege of an only once-read newspaper, for at seven pence they were frequently passed along several people.

"Mrs Harcourt?" Diana recalled the name but not the lady. She knew her to be an old acquaintance of her mother's, but their circumstances had forced them out of her society.

"She is in Bath, I believe, and may have some notion of how we might manage all this."

Diana was reluctant to approach anyone whom she considered to have shunned them, and said so. But her mother assuaged her concerns.

"My dear, it was nothing of the sort, though you were too young to remember. Jocasta went to Scotland shortly before your father's death. We have stayed in touch these many years, though I am not as diligent a letter writer as I should be. Both her daughters have made successful marriages and her son is an officer in the navy. She last wrote that she planned to return south with her husband. Should she be in Bath, as she mentioned, she will be an excellent person to advise us."

The flock of rare Cotswold long horns turned out to be as much of a blessing as their accompanying fortune, in Diana's opinion. For Mrs St Clair, despite her gentle nature, was unyielding when it came to matters of duty. She was adamant that the sheep should not be sold.

"Our cousin's greatest concern was for the welfare of his flock. I shall do my best to uphold his wishes," she told her daughters.

"Surely we could find some accommodating farmer with a spare field?" Henrietta suggested.

But Mrs St Clair insisted that the sheep must be pastured in the family's vicinity.

While her sisters were frustrated, Diana was only too happy to support her mother in this view. For it meant that they must find a country house rather than a town house, and this would suit her mother's health best.

A suitable residence was soon found. This was a small but beautifully proportioned house set among orchards, at the foot of a grassy hill not three miles from Bath. "It is almost too perfect," Diana said. "You may look out of your window at your flock grazing, mamma." She arranged for the hiring of a shepherd, a local mazed boy who could not speak but had an instinct with animals.

There was much to do in preparing the new home, organising furniture and servants. The St Clairs had only been able to keep one servant, an able girl named Ellen. She had served as both cook and parlourmaid, assisted by a charwoman from the village.

All the activity meant that Diana was too busy to involve herself in the ordering of clothes. This task fell instead to Henrietta. Jocasta Harcourt had been of enormous help in recommending a talented seamstress. This clever woman was able to create a sufficient wardrobe for all three young women to enter society with the least delay.

The generous Mrs Harcourt, aware of her friend's health, also offered to chaperone the sisters. "They may stay with me and Mr Harcourt in Bath, Catherine dear. I will take them to the assemblies and guide them through the whirl of activity. For three young heiresses, not to mention such charming girls as your daughters, are sure to be an object of great interest and demand."

This was of great relief to everyone.

When the first batch of gowns arrived, Diana was horrified by the garments presented to her. She had requested fabrics in delicate shades of white, cream and palest rose, suitable for a girl in her first real season. To her dismay she found vivid hues of jonquil and puce. Diana was not by nature vain but she was aware that these colours were not becoming to her.

"How could you order such garish colours for me?" she demanded of Henrietta.

Her sister's air of indignation masked guilt. "And how do you suppose we might have looked, Maria and I, trailing a young miss in white muslin? Would you have us derided as your two elderly spinster sisters? We have already suffered the inequity of years of seclusion through penury, yet you enjoy the privilege of moving straight from the schoolroom into society."

Diana was forced to concede there was some truth in this. Though she rejected any idea that her sisters might be taken as elderly, or spinsters. "Even Maria is not yet five-and-twenty. Many women do not marry until such an age. Indeed I have even heard it said that a woman does not reach her true radiance until thirty."

Henrietta was little mollified by this. "Then you may be gratified that the colours I have chosen for you will make you look less maidenly," was her retort. "Besides, we may surely order a hundred more gowns should we wish."

The long-horned sheep finally arrived, bleating and jostling as they were unloaded from the cart. Henrietta, who had fancied a flock of snow white lambs, was disappointed by the shaggy beasts with their unkempt, greyish fleeces. "Some of them be lambing the next few months, milady," the man driving the carts reassured her.

Maria was indifferent, other than to remark that the sheep appeared to be healthy and robust looking animals. Diana found herself taken with the two large rams, which sported enormous curling horns. "Do they have names, do you think?" she pondered. "I wonder if it would be irreverent to christen them Lord Henry and Lord Harrogate?"

"Indeed it would," her mother replied, suppressing a smile. "I do not know if one names sheep. They are larger than I had anticipated. We all have much to learn about their species and its husbandry."

Maria had no interest in doing so. "I do not think you need concern yourself with such details, Mamma. Let the shepherd boy attend to them."

But Diana considered that the sheep might become an engaging area of interest for her mother. "We shall order you a silver crook in Bath," she vowed, at which both her sisters and mother laughed.

The days of penury, those long, monotonous days where the future seemed bleak and unchanging, were over. Next week they would join the throng of the bon ton in Bath. And if that city did not enjoy the prestige and highest of society as London did, it might yet be viewed as a rehearsal for the St Clair sisters' eventual arrival on the London scene.

CHAPTER 2

The Duke of Eastleigh's attention was briefly captured by the young woman across the room. His first impression was of gleaming gold hair and a startlingly pure line of feature. But this was quickly overwhelmed as he took in the wider scene.

The Duke was not a man of fashion but he was a man of refinement. Having been struck by her beauty, he was now struck by the vulgarity of her gown, both in colour and style. He must have been mistaken in his first impression of her being of young age, for no debutante would be permitted to wear such a garment.

The two women she stood with were little better. Worse, in fact. But what pained the Duke the most was that his young cousin Frederick stood with them, engaged in quite ostentatious flirtation. Had he no better sense than to associate with vulgar chits such as these?

Not wishing to approach any closer, he spoke to the man who accompanied him. "Retrieve my cousin if you would, Monty. Inform him that if he is not ready to leave this rout within five minutes, I shall not instruct Ayrdale to sell him those two black stallions."

Confident that this threat would do the trick, with the stallions holding more appeal than the society of silly women, the Duke watched his friend cross the floor towards the group. Montague Chalmers, a far more amiable person than his nobler friend, was used to this kind of request. Eastleigh frequently chose not to engage directly with people but sent Monty, or whoever else was available, to carry his message.

Or rather, his commands, Monty thought. He did not

however resent the Duke's high handed approach. Over the years he had become accustomed to it and judged that it stemmed from uncertainty as much as reserve. He had known Eastleigh for many years. He considered him a generous and steadfast friend, despite his austere and frequently autocratic demeanour.

James Beresford, Duke of Eastleigh had reached the age of seven-and-thirty still unencumbered by a wife. This might have been remarkable given his title, wealth and noble bearing. But the Duke had determined to marry by his fortieth birthday and not too long beforehand. He viewed marriage and the subsequent begetting of an heir as one of the many duties required by his position. It should be with a woman of impeccable character and lineage, appropriate for the role of Duchess of Eastleigh.

He had several candidates vaguely in mind. None of them held much personal interest for him, but all came from families that would represent a favourable political alliance.

At the top of this list was a Lady Jane Hampton, daughter of John Hampton, Earl Amberforth. Lady Jane was known to be very devout. The Duke was not overly religious himself, but he considered it a potentially desirable quality in a spouse.

It was on this marital mission that he had found himself in Bath. There were details to go over with Amberforth, who had indicated he was not opposed to the union. The presence of the Duke's wayward nephew was an unwelcome complication. He had promised his sister to look out for the boy. Yet as he watched his nephew revelling in the society of vulgarly dressed young women, the Duke was already regretting his promise.

Approaching the group, Montague Chalmers bowed to the three women addressed them and the Hon. Frederick Fulham. "I beg your pardon for interrupting, but I bear a message from your cousin. I have not yet the pleasure of your acquaintance?"

he said, having turned to the St Clair sisters.

The Hon. Frederick looked over his shoulder where the Duke was standing towards the back of the room. His countenance was impassive, though Frederick knew his cousin well enough to detect some irritation. He made the appropriate introductions, after which he picked up the previous thread of conversation. "As I was saying, at the Beaumonts' ball last month..."

Monty cleared his throat. "I do regret to remind you, but your cousin was quite insistent."

"Confound it and confound him," Frederick exclaimed. "You may tell him that I am currently engaged in conversation. Since there appears to be no urgency, I will join him when I am free."

Monty played his one trump card. "His Grace did mention something regarding Ayrdale's stallions."

Now Frederick was the one to look irritated. In his early twenties, and as aimless as he was amiable, he had a weakness for racing. His heart was set on the stallions for a new phaeton that his mother had been indulgent enough to buy for him.

These delightful women could wait, he reasoned. They had indicated they would be in Bath for the rest of the season. And besides, there were any number of pretty young women in town. But only one pair of gleaming black steeds that would absolutely see him beat Albemarle the next time they met.

"Very well," he said. He made polite apologies to Maria, Henrietta and Diana. "My cousin summons me, I fear. That's him over there. He's a beastly bore and as stuffy as anything but you know how it is with dukes."

The St Clair sisters had no notion of how it was with Dukes, or any other nobly titled gentlemen. But Maria, as the eldest, accepted his departure with grace and expressed hope that they might meet again on a future.

"By all means," Frederick said with some enthusiasm. He

returned to his cousin with Monty, equally apologetic and bowing again as they left.

Diana had noticed the tall, dark man at the back of the hall. Exquisitely dressed and extremely handsome, she had fancied for a moment that he had caught her eye. But just as quickly he looked away again. Most likely he was keeping an eye on his young cousin, she decided.

She glanced once more in his direction as the men exited, noting the perfect shape of his head, the black hair closely cropped, revealing the sculptured lines of his neck above his stiff white collar. It was too much to expect that the St Clairs should mingle with dukes, she supposed, heiresses or not.

"What a very charming man," Henrietta said, fanning herself. "How delightful his conversation was. I believe he was genuinely regretful to depart from us. I suppose a duke's request cannot be ignored."

"Certainly," Maria agreed, having no better idea as to the nature of a duke's request than her sister.

Only Diana wondered at the Duke's sending of another man - albeit a very personable one - to recover his cousin. She could not help but feel that it seemed high-handed. As noble as he was, and as fine his features were, there had nonetheless been a trace of arrogance in his demeanour.

The sisters rejoined Jocasta Harcourt who had been engaged in conversation with an old acquaintance. Mr Harcourt, who disliked the crush at the Assembly Rooms, had declined to accompany the party that day.

Mrs Harcourt welcomed the three girls and inquired as to their progress. She had been delighted by the chance to chaperone them. She had missed the intrigue and gossip of the marriage market since her own two daughters had successfully graduated from it.

"I trust you are all enjoying yourselves?" she asked.

"Very much so. We have been in conversation with the

cousin of a duke!" Henrietta announced.

"Indeed? And which duke might that be?"

Henrietta had to confess that they did not know. Some detective work on the part of Mrs Harcourt established that this was likely the Duke of Eastleigh. "A very wealthy and noble man, my dears, and as yet unmarried." She spoke in jest, for a duke must certainly be beyond the ambitions of most young women present. However fair and well-dowried they were.

"Unmarried!" Henrietta had no such modesty when it came to her own ambitions. "But he is not a young man, surely? There is perhaps some tragic mystery there?"

Mrs Harcourt laughed. "None that I am aware of. Gentlemen may have the luxury of choosing when they wed. They do not wilt and fade as a rose in autumn, as we unfortunate women do. But you are all in your springtime," she added hastily. She was aware that both Maria and Henrietta had made their debut several seasons ago and might be sensitive on the subject of time. She was fond of all three girls, partly due to her admiration and long acquaintance with their mother. But Maria's excellent manners, Henrietta's eagerness and interest, and Diana's quiet grace all held their appeal. Jocasta Harcourt was confident that they all stood a good chance of making commendable matches.

"Perhaps the Duke may be here in Bath to finally make his choice?" Henrietta suggested with some hope.

"According to rumour he is all but betrothed to Earl Amberforth's daughter."

Diana, who had felt irrationally uplifted on hearing that the Duke was unmarried, felt a sinking at this news.

"What is she like?" Henrietta asked. "Is she very beautiful?"

Mrs Harcourt confessed that she had seen the young woman in question on but one occasion. "It was at a ball during my youngest daughter's first season. She was pointed out to me. As I recall she was very well dressed, but quite reserved."

Henrietta wrinkled her small nose. "I declare I loathe her already!" she announced. "Only imagine being a duchess! It seems most unfair that such a privilege should be afforded to someone who is already the daughter of an earl."

Maria chided her, fearful they might be overheard. "It may well be a love match," she suggested.

Mrs Harcourt, worldly enough to be rather more cynical about such affairs, was not wholehearted in agreement. "Maybe so, maybe so. Now I am sure we have all stood too long on our feet, and you must be in need of refreshments. Let us see if we may take tea. Then we will return home, for doubtless you will want time to dress for the dancing tonight."

CHAPTER 3

The following morning Diana accompanied Mrs Harcourt on an errand in town. Her sisters, claiming exhaustion from the dancing the previous night, had not yet risen.

It had rained earlier but the sun had now broken through, and the streets of Bath were bright and bathed with gold. The milliner's shop where Mrs Harcourt was purchasing gloves was crowded with people, so Diana remained outside. As she waited, she caught sight of a familiar face.

"Mary Elford!"

"Miss Diana!"

The two young women greeted one another in delight. Mary Elford was the daughter of the vicar in the village where the St Clairs had formerly lived. Only a year older than Maria, she had been engaged as their governess. Sadly even her meagre wage had been a strain on the family's purse. Eventually, when Maria and Henrietta outgrew the schoolroom, Mrs St Clair had been forced to let Mary go.

Diana had missed her most of all. Despite the gap in years between the two girls, Mary had been as a sister to her. More so than her actual sisters, for she and Mary had shared a love of nature, of reading and of history.

"But how you are grown! And become so lovely!" Mary laughed. "I dare say I make myself sound very elderly, saying such. But I am an old married woman myself now." The merry twinkle in her eye and the healthy glow in her cheeks bore strong witness against such a description.

"Of course! I had forgotten that you are married," Diana said.

"Yes. I am no longer Mary Elford, the Reverend Elford's

daughter, but Mrs Matthew Hollis. And we have a son, William, just past his first birthday."

Diana expressed congratulations and said how very happy they had all been to hear the news. "We were so sorry to part company with you." She remembered the time when Mary had departed. It had followed a bitterly cold winter where Mrs St Clair had struggled to buy enough firewood to keep their cottage warm. The damp had seeped into all their bones and there had been doctors' bills to pay. A terrible influenza had swept the village, taking several of the elderly and frail. Mrs St Clair herself had been much weakened by it.

Both were silent for a moment, remembering that difficult time.

"But I understand you have recently come into much happier circumstances?" Mary said. "My father wrote to tell me. I am so very glad for you all. How is your mother's health?"

"I believe it is already improved," Diana said. "I am hopeful that the better air of our new house will do much to restore her. Did you hear that we are now the guardians of a flock of rare sheep?"

Mary had heard this. "With golden fleeces, according to rumours in the parish."

Diana laughed. "With shaggy and unkempt fleeces, but I dare say they will be washed to snow white at spinning time. Tell me more of your marriage and your husband."

Blushing, Mary began a glowing description of her husband, before hesitating. "He is in trade, of course…" She trailed off, embarrassed.

"What is the problem with that?" Diana asked.

Mary tried to explain. "It is not of the station of your sisters and yourself, of course." Marriage to a man in business had cemented her rank as below that that of the St Clairs.

Diana dismissed this qualm. "But he is a good man, and his work his honest?" she asked, to which her friend nodded.

"Then I do not see the problem. I would far rather take an honest tradesman as husband than" - Diana cast around for some antithesis to this - "an arrogant Duke."

Now it was Mary's turn to laugh. "Would that one were faced with such a choice!"

As she spoke, Diana spied a tall man striding along the opposite side of the street. His height. bearing and the flawless cut of his clothing set him apart from the other passers-by. Speak of the devil, she thought. And at that moment his gaze fell across the street and onto her. She quickly looked away, grateful for the noise of the crowds and carriages. Imagine if he had heard her!

Mary was looking hesitantly at Diana again. "We leave Bath tomorrow, which I am now very sorry for as I would dearly love to meet with you and your sisters and learn more of your news. I do not suppose, if you are ever in London, you might be willing to pay us a visit? We live not far from St James's Park. Our house is well appointed, though not grand."

"I would dearly love to visit," Diana said. "I know no one in London though, so I cannot say if or when I will be there."

Mary hesitated again. "If your mamma would not regard it unsuitable, we would be delighted if you would stay with us. Your sisters too, if they might wish it. We would be so very honoured to have you."

Diana smiled. "'I would be equally delighted to come, on one condition. That you welcome me as a sister, and not as some honoured guest. For I should find it a horrible strain to be on my best behaviour every moment. We were as sisters before, and your marriage and our altered circumstances make no difference to that."

Her friend was relieved and moved. "You sound very old and wise for your years. It is a trait I remember from your schoolroom days."

Mrs Harcourt emerged at this point, laden with her

purchases. Diana made introductions. "A charming young woman," was Mrs Harcourt's verdict once Mary had departed. "A vicar's daughter, you say? I warrant she has done better than to marry the curate, judging by her clothes."

Diana, who unlike Henrietta was not so observant as to dress, asked what Mrs Harcourt meant by this.

"Only that her cape was of a very fine quality. It would not look out of place on a countess," Jocasta Harcourt explained as they walked back to the Harcourts' house.

This brought Diana to a subject she had been longing to address. "I hope you will not think me indulgent, but I am wanting to make some remedy to my wardrobe," she began. "As you know we were in a great rush to prepare everything for our visit here. Some of the fabrics and styles did not turn out quite as I had desired."

A mystery was solved for Mrs Harcourt. She had wondered at the choices of colour and excessive ornaments for Diana's gowns. The girl was only seventeen and they were far from the styles that Mrs Harcourt would have dressed her own daughters in at that age. She had assumed that Diana had chosen through inexperience or poor taste. It was a relief to discover this was not the case.

"Certainly we can engage a modiste, should you wish. I do not think that your mother would object, for she instructed me to ensure that you were fully fitted out for the season."

Diana, also relieved, thanked Mrs Harcourt as the two of them arrived back. Mrs Harcourt departed to put her purchases away and give instructions to the cook for a dinner party she was hosting the following evening.

The Duke of Eastleigh had recognised the young woman across the street. Once again the gleam of gold under her bonnet and the grace of her profile momentarily transfixed him. She was better dressed this morning, though he barely noticed her clothes this time.

He saw her laugh at a comment made by the woman she was conversing with. It gave him an odd pang of regret that he was not the one to have made her laugh.

As if reading his mind, she looked over at him then but quickly averted her gaze.

The Duke recovered himself. What was he thinking? He had no time for foolish young women who spent their time chattering in the street and berated himself for his mental lapse. He was on his way to call on Amberforth and had declined to take a carriage. Walking was better for the constitution.

The Earl of Amberforth's Bath residence was a large villa built on neo-Classical lines. It was a more convenient distance from his country estate than London, so he was more often to be found there.

Admitted by a footman, the Duke was shown into the library where Amberforth rose to greet him.

"Eastleigh. Good of you to come. Come alone, have you?"

The Duke's propensity to travel without servants was known. Dukes could afford their eccentricities, of course. The two men discussed some matters of business, including the proposed matrimonials. Amberforth, being neither a snob nor in need of money, was equanimous as to whether the match occurred. If Jane were favourable to a proposal he had no objection. If she rejected a suitor, even a duke, her father was satisfied that she knew her own mind and had no wish to force her.

For his part he liked Eastleigh well enough, though considered the man rather a cold fish. That might suit Jane though, the girl was remarkably reserved. "You'll want to call in on Jane for a moment?" he asked, wondering if it should perhaps have been Eastleigh's first priority.

"If she is able to receive me," the Duke said.

He was ushered into a morning room, where the pale grey

stripe of the walls and silver velvet of the upholstery created a sepulchral effect. Jane rose when he entered and curtseyed. "Your Grace."

She wore a simple muslin morning dress, plain not sprigged, with a small pearl cross around her neck. In her left hand she clasped a psalter, bound in white kid, that she placed on the table next to her chair.

The Duke, worldly enough in his own way and perfectly capable of conversation with anyone from a prince to a peddler, found himself at a loss for words. Jane waited patiently, her even features serene. For the first time the Duke of Eastleigh wondered if this detached formality between them was in fact desirable in a matrimonial union. They must beget an heir, after all.

He tried imagining the woman before him placed in his bedchamber, perhaps in some white robe, her brown hair spilling over the pillows. It was a difficult image to summon. It was not helped by the sudden fancy of another young woman lying there instead, with golden hair and a laughing intelligence in her eyes.

"You are aware," he began, "that I have discussed with your father a possible marriage between us?"

"I am, sir." Her expression remained impassive.

"I trust that you would not object to such a union?"

She replied in the same, calm tone. "Not if my father wishes it, sir."

But what do *you* wish? the Duke thought, feeling a surge of frustration. Should they marry, he would face this taciturn woman each day: dining with her, raising children with her. Might the marriage night awaken some more energetic feeling in her? In both of them? He quailed at the prospect if it did not.

Perhaps she was shy. "I am in no haste, my dear, should you require time to become accustomed to the idea. There is no pressing need to announce or formalise a betrothal." Was he buying time for her or for himself?

The Duke thought he detected relief in her face, but perhaps it was his own fancy. His own wish to see relief there. For if she were reluctant, he would cease all further negotiations without rancour.

He should have brought Monty with him. Monty had a gift for this sort of thing. Putting women at their ease. Relaxing even the most reticent or nervous of maidens and engaging them in conversation. It was a skill that the Duke had rather disdained than approved before, but at this painful point he would have welcomed it.

Because it was painful. Neither of them wanted to be here, in one another's company, holding this awkward discourse.

He took his leave with as much grace as he could muster and fled, still unresolved as to what to do.

CHAPTER 4

Maria and Henrietta had been invited out by some new friends the following evening. Diana declined to go, preferring to remain with the Harcourts and attend their dinner party. "It is only a small affair of old friends," Jocasta Harcourt had told her. "I dare say you will find them all very elderly and stuffy. But if you were to come, we will have even numbers for whist."

Diana, who could not face another night in jonquil, was more than glad to do so. She had not greatly taken to Lucy Beasley or her sister Mrs Petersham. That Mrs Harcourt welcomed her presence to make up the numbers strengthened her resolve to stay.

"I cannot think why you choose to remain behind," Maria remarked. "Miss Beasley and her sister are very well connected in Bath society. They have promised to introduce us to the very best people."

"Then you may introduce me to them once you enjoy the same acquaintance," Diana replied.

Henrietta found herself ambivalent as to her younger sister accompanying them. On one hand she felt that three sisters presented far more of a spectacle than two. But on the other hand, she had become increasingly aware that Diana had blossomed in a manner that threatened to rival her own attractions. Diana's hair might not curl, but it was an eye-catching gold, and her silver-grey eyes and even features might well be regarded as beautiful.

Deciding that such competition was a disadvantage, Henrietta did not protest her sister's absence. She busied herself choosing a gown and accoutrements, and having the maid attend to her hair. This was a luxury that Henrietta revelled in. She had suffered the less dextrous attempts of her sisters over the years, and the results had frequently pained her. "We will be sure to bring you an account of anyone interesting," she promised her youngest sister.

While her sisters readied themselves Diana wrote a letter to her mother. She needed little time herself to dress for dinner. Mrs Harcourt had lent her a Spanish shawl to mask the worst of the puce gown. Diana was hopeful that by candlelight its gaudy pink hue might be softened further.

Diana's letters were filled with spirit and amusing anecdotes of their time in Bath. A naturally engaging correspondent, she had the gift of turning the most mundane social event into a fascinating intrigue and making a witty caricature of the dullest of people. She was never unkind, but she was observant. If she allowed herself a little exaggeration, her conscience was assuaged by the fact that the persons in question would never read it.

As a result the Honourable Frederick Fulham became even more eager and foppish, and his noble cousin all the more stiff-lipped and haughty. *"I am sure that the Duke quite disdained us at the Assembly rooms,"* Diana wrote, *"for he would not even approach our group, but instead sent some other man to command his relative's return. I caught sight of him in the street the following day and he looked no less formidable. They say he is to marry an Earl's daughter. I can only say that I am very glad myself not to have been born to such high rank and have such a husband forced upon me."*

Of the former Mary Elford, now Mrs Hollis, she wrote in glowing terms. She expressed how well Mary looked, and passed on her best wishes to her mother. *"I have not yet met her husband but he sounds a fine man, and Mary is eager for me to visit them in London. They have a house near St James's Park. It is a good area of town, is it not? I hope you will have no objections, mamma, since I am keen to accept their kind invitation."*

At dinner Diana found that she was to be seated between Colonel Arbuthnot, a retired military gentleman with large moustaches, and Mr Grange, a scholarly man in his late forties with a surprisingly vivacious wife. This lady was one of Mrs Harcourt's dearest friends. Diana was glad to make her acquaintance.

"But she is quite a beauty, Jocasta!" Mrs Grange exclaimed after being introduced to Diana and having had the St Clairs' circumstances explained to her. This was uttered within earshot of Diana. She blushed and tried to conceal the fact that she had overheard. "Who did you say her mother is?" Mrs Grange asked.

Mrs Harcourt had not yet disclosed this. "Catherine Harborough. A dear friend of mine from girlhood."

"I do recall the name. A beauty herself, was she not? I should think you will have no trouble marrying the girl off by the end of the month. With those looks and a fortune! The dullest debutante could not fail to make a match with such assets."

Diana, having grown up with her sister acknowledged as the pretty one, was unused to such flattering words. She felt greatly embarrassed. But when Mrs Grange engaged her in conversation, she found that woman so merry and effervescent that she was all the more pleased to have made a good impression on her.

"You will find London very much more of a whirl than Bath," Mrs Grange said, on hearing of Diana's plans to visit a friend there. "Should you wish to make a match this season, you will find very many more eligible young men in the capital. All the more so if you can obtain vouchers to Almack's."

Diana declined to mention that her friends were not members of the ton. There was no chance whatsoever the Hollises would be admitted to those fashionable assembly rooms. "I am not sure if I wish to marry," she said.

Mrs Grange took this to mean that Diana did not intend to marry yet. "You are one of these modern girls who prefers to wait a couple of seasons? There may well be something to be said for delay. For I do not know that I have ever enjoyed myself as much as during that time. All the balls and the dancing and the delicious rivalry! Though there is much to be said for marriage as well. More to be said, in fact. It is a state of exquisite felicity!"

Glancing over at the sombre Mr Grange, such a contrast to the vivacity of his wife, Diana marvelled at how this might be so. She was no less enlightened when it was her turn to converse with him at dinner. The Colonel was a distinctly more engaging conversationalist, regaling Diana with tales of his exploits in foreign places. These were quite thrilling. All the more so as the claret loosened Colonel Arbuthnot's tongue.

It was with some regret that Diana struggled to converse with Mr Grange on the possibility of revisions to the Book of Common Prayer. She longed to join in a conversation that Mr Harcourt was having on the Corn Laws at the other end of the table. It was an issue she had followed closely, due to its impact on the St Clairs' investments. Though these were small beer now, Diana supposed, since Lord Harrogate's legacy.

As she strained to follow the thread of conversation while continuing to make polite murmurs of agreement to Mr Grange, her ears caught the name "Amberforth".

"I bumped into Amberforth at my club earlier," an elderly gentleman was saying. "Got his eldest all but engaged to Eastleigh, by all accounts."

"Eastleigh must be getting on a bit these days," the woman next to him replied. "About time he turned his efforts towards succession."

"A good catch for Amberforth at any rate. Though he's as rich as Croesus himself."

His neighbour asked whether anyone knew anything of the

prospective bride.

"A very demure woman," the elderly gentleman informed them. "No longer in her first youth, of course."

"All to the better," Mrs Grange interrupted. "At his age, he should hardly be dallying with debutants. I don't hold with these Winter-Spring affairs. Only look at Ponsonby and the fool she made of him."

The conversation was taking a thrillingly scandalous turn for Diana, who scarcely dared breathe lest someone remembered her more tender ears. There were matters that married people discussed that were not considered fit for maidens. She longed to know what had happened with the Ponsonby marriage but dared not ask, and nothing further enlightening was said.

Nor was anything more mentioned on the subject when the ladies retired after dinner. Mrs Grange led much of the conversation. She was very well acquainted with all the goings on in town, and appeared to know everyone, either directly or through a connection.

Diana decided to be bold. "The Duke of Eastleigh was mentioned at dinner," she said, and then wondered at her own fascination with the man. It was probably because she had fancied he had looked upon her. Albeit with a very disapproving eye.

Mrs Grange was flattered to be consulted about the nobility and shared what she knew. "By all accounts he is a very staid and austere man, so doubtless the match with Lady Jane will be a suitable one. Though I have it from a highly reliable source that he fought a duel in his youth, for the sake of a lady's honour. That suggests a more passionate nature, does it not?"

Diana agreed that it did.

"I do not think I should like to have a duel fought over me," Mrs Grange continued. "One would feel terrible guilt if either gentleman were injured."

"Like Helen of Troy?" Diana suggested, but Mrs Grange was not a classical scholar.

"It may well be so," was her only remark. At that point they were interrupted by a summons to rejoin the gentleman and form whist tables. Diana, who was not seated in the same foursome as Mrs Grange, had to be content with the Colonel again.

CHAPTER 5

The Duke remained troubled following his interview with Lady Jane Amberforth. To distract himself he arranged to dine that night with Montague Chalmers. This was an error, because Monty immediately detected that something was wrong.

"Something on your mind, Eastleigh?"

The Duke was not a man who prevaricated. While private by instinct, he had on more than one occasion found Montague a valuable source of advice. "Arranging matrimony has turned out to be more complex than I had anticipated."

Monty assumed that his friend referred to legal issues. "There is some dispute over the settlement?"

"No, not that at all." The Duke took a draught of his wine. "I am concerned that the lady in question is not as favourably minded towards the union as might have been expected."

"It must have rather disrupted her plans," Monty agreed.

The Duke was startled. "Her plans?"

Now Monty was disconcerted. Surely Eastleigh was aware of his chosen bride's intense piety. "Supposedly she wished to take orders a year or so ago. But Amberforth wouldn't hear of it."

"Orders? You mean holy orders?"

"Indeed."

It took the Duke some moments to absorb this. Certainly it put a very different complexion on the whole affair. A devout wife was one thing, but one whose true desire was for the cloisters was beyond the pale. "If that is so, it may not be the most appropriate course to pursue this." Inwardly he felt relief at Monty's revelation rather than dismay.

The two men continued their meal in silence for some time. Montague knew that Eastleigh needed time to consider this new information and waited for him to resume the conversation.

After the servant cleared the dishes for that course, the Duke spoke again. "I have never considered affairs of passion a wise basis for a marriage."

"No," Monty agreed. "Perhaps finding a balance may be the wisest course, though."

"A balance?"

Monty chose his words carefully. "A warm friendship and mutual regard, at the very least." In truth Monty was a romantic at heart. He could not imagine contemplating marriage unless he was utterly dazzled by a girl. But he did not have a duchy to consider, nor, being wealthy, a dowry. "There is a risk," he elaborated, "that such a friendship might not develop after marriage."

This was exactly the Duke's hesitation when it came to Amberforth's daughter. Having sat in awkward conversation with her, he realised such discomfort was not a prospect he relished in his own home, year after year. One might manage to live a separate life from one's spouse, and this was something he had anticipated doing himself. But there would be times when husband and wife were forced into proximity, and at these times companionability would be desirable.

Monty, who had never considered the Duke's choice of the Amberforth girl very favourably, was heartened to think that his friend might be reconsidering the match. A wife would be good for him, Monty thought, but it needed to be the right kind of woman. A meek and retiring female, which appeared to be Eastleigh's aim, would be the worst kind of spouse. He needed someone with sufficient spine and spirit to shake him out of his solemnity and lighten his mood.

"There were other names on your list," Monty said. It had

not been a written list, but Eastleigh had discussed other prospects with him. "Was not Wilde's daughter among them?" The raven-haired Isabella Wilde had been judged a diamond of the first water in her debut season. Inexplicably she had rejected suitor after suitor.

Raven hair was not in the Duke's mind at that precise moment. The vision of a golden head still lingered.

Diana had made one good friend of her own since arriving in Bath. Susannah Lewis was the granddaughter of a wealthy industrialist and her mother was the youngest daughter of a baronet. Despite this, she was on occasion slighted by those who considered the Lewises to be of inferior rank.

Diana had been privy to such a conversation while in the Pump Room one morning. Sitting behind the screen of potted palm, two voices had carried to her ears. "We must invite the Beaumonts and the Debenhams. And the Feversham sisters. The Lewis girl? Good heavens, no! Her clothes may be ostentatiously expensive, but her family owns mills."

"Something to do with iron, is it not?"

"Metals - mills - mines - what difference does it make?"

Derisive laughter followed.

It was such a spiteful and unjust verdict - for Diana had met Miss Lewis and did not consider her wardrobe in any way ostentatious - that she was highly tempted to berate the two women for their snobbery. Realising that this would bring embarrassment upon Mrs Harcourt, she held her tongue. Instead she rose from her seat, and making her presence very apparent, strode past the women refusing to even look at them.

After this incident she sought Susannah Lewis out, and soon found that they shared a true accord. Susannah was only a year older than Diana and had a keen intelligence and a lively sense of fun. She also had the gift of turning misfortune into an advantage.

"I am well aware that people shun me because of how my grandfather made his money," she confided in Diana one day. "It serves as a wonderful filter, sparing me from the worst snobs and bores."

Despite her family's lowly origins, Susannah did not want for suitors. With her ebony hair and alabaster skin - at least this was the description given by one poetical swain - she was greatly in demand among the young bucks and hopefuls.

"My cousin Charles will be in Bath next week," she revealed to Diana when they stopped for refreshments at one of the many dances. "I should so like you to make his acquaintance."

"I would be delighted to," Diana replied. Susannah had mentioned her cousin before. The son of her father's elder brother, he managed the family business. "Only I leave Bath for London next Friday. I hope that we will still have time to meet."

Susannah was sure it would be possible. "He will come to the Assembly Rooms, so there will be ample opportunity."

As they discussed plans, and the various invitations they had received, Diana recalled a subject that still intrigued her. "Did you ever hear of some people by the name of Ponsonby?"

Susannah's eyes widened and she drew closer. "Do you refer to the Ponsonby scandal?"

Diana supposed that she did.

Susannah spoke in hushed tones, her dark eyes gleaming with excitement. "I am sure that we ought not to speak of it, but it is so thrilling a tale. He was well past his fiftieth birthday and very wealthy. She was but nineteen and very beautiful, so they say, but not a penny to her name. They married, and that was considered quite scandalous enough, I believe."

"It was not a love match, then?" Diana asked.

Susannah nearly convulsed with mirth. "Not at all! He was very stout, with a face like a boiled haddock, so I heard one of my mother's friends describe him. I was not supposed to be listening, of course. And she, as I have said, was very fair. Anyway, they were wed, and within a twelvemonth she had taken up with some French émigré and fled to the continent!"

"They were banished there?"

Susannah shook her head. "Not so. She went quite of her own accord, and I can only suppose she lives there to this day. This happened about a year ago."

Diana felt sympathy for both parties. Mr Ponsonby's humiliation must have been all the greater, due to his folly. And she thought, with something of a shudder, how near she or one of her sisters might have come to such a circumstance. She knew that her mother had rejected a couple of suitors for Henrietta, one of whom had been quite elderly. Had poverty gripped the St Clairs even harder, might Henrietta have been forced to accept such a fate?

Diana's sisters chided her for her intimacy with Susannah Lewis. "She is not at all well-connected and it is all new money," Maria said.

Diana pointed out that the St Clair's money was even newer.

"That is not at all the same, as you are well aware. Our family is a very ancient and noble one. Briefly distressed circumstances do not negate that."

How Maria could dismiss their years of hardship, and what their mother in particular had suffered, as "briefly distressed" irritated Diana. It only strengthened her resolve to ignore Maria's unwelcome advice. Besides which, from her regular reading of the newspaper, Diana was aware that the *nouveau riche* were increasingly accepted in society. Rich merchants and commercial magnates appeared in the lists of guests at the finest houses, and their sons and daughters intermarried with the aristocracy on a frequent basis. St Clair Hall itself had been bought by a successful industrialist.

Her sisters also disapproved of Diana's plans to stay with Mary Hollis and expressed no wish to take up the invitation themselves. "I hardly think a vicar's daughter, married to a tradesman, will be of any help in entering London society."

"That is not my purpose in staying with the Hollises," Diana said.

Mrs Harcourt had no such objection to Diana associating with Miss Lewis or her plans to visit her friends in London, should her mother be favourable. Mrs Harcourt's husband's mother was French and had fled the Revolution. Mrs Harcourt was thus aware of the plight of many aristocratic émigrés, forced to work as seamstresses and run lodging houses. Thus she shared Diana's views on the dignity of honest toil.

"It is indeed a changing world we live in. A collier might buy himself a castle and have a count sweep his floors." With her daughters safely married off - not to colliers - and her husband and herself in a very comfortable situation, Mrs Harcourt could afford to be phlegmatic.

The following week Susannah met Diana in the Pump Room, accompanied by a very pleasant-looking young man whom she introduced as her cousin. Mr Charles Lewis was five-and-twenty. He had excellent features, a healthy complexion and an appealing manner. Diana found him very charming.

She had wondered if Susannah harboured a fondness for her cousin that went beyond familial feeling. Certainly her friend's descriptions of him had been numerous and favourable. But on encountering them together, Diana detected nothing more than a sisterly fondness.

"How you are liking Bath, Miss St Clair?" Charles Lewis asked, after introductions were made.

"I am enjoying myself very much. All the more so since I have been fortunate enough to make Miss Lewis's acquaintance," Diana said.

Susannah was amused. "I do think we may do away with convention, Charles, if Miss St Clair is not opposed. For we have been on first name terms ourselves for some time now. What would you say to the same? At least when we are among ourselves."

Charles Lewis expressed that he would be delighted, if Diana did not find it an imposition. Diana did not.

Having taken the waters, which they all considered distinctly unpleasant regardless of any claimed health properties, they departed the Pump Room and took a short stroll towards Milsom Street. Here was a fashionable confectioners filled with delights ample to obliterate all memory of the water.

Diana, for whom confectionery was still a delicious novelty, struggled with such an array of choice. She deferred to her friends, who bought a large selection of sweetmeats. They feasted on violet macaroons, fancy rout cakes and rosewater jellies, with conversation as sparkling as the victuals were sweet.

Charles spoke about his work in such detail that his cousin finally protested. "I am sure Diana does not wish to be educated in the intricacies of smelting processes! Only let us talk on a more interesting subject."

"What would you have in mind? I am sure you must be sick of gossip and scandal, having spent so long amid Bath's polite society. Which, as we all know, is anything but," Charles teased her.

Susannah declared that she would enjoy nothing better. "So much is kept from us here. Yet I cannot see how our ears may be any more delicate than yours."

Charles gestured for the attendant to bring them another jug of capillaire. It was a syrup that was rather too sweet for Diana, who would have preferred tea. "I doubt I have any gossip that you would consider worthwhile. I can tell you how much Mickelson lost at poker last night, or what Harry Tanqueray wagered when he raced Barham over the Iron Bridge."

"Those are not at all interesting or even scandalous," Susannah chided him. "We wish to know what peer has proposed to an actress, or what duchess has disgraced herself with the footman."

"I'm afraid you have the wrong fellow for that, cousin dear," Charles said. "Besides which, those are not matters that us gentlemen discuss anyway."

Susannah dismissed this. "Fie! You gossip at your clubs just as much as any old women around the faro table. It was you who told me about the Ponsonbys, was it not?"

"Everyone knows about the Ponsonbys. A blind man might have predicted that conclusion," her cousin observed.

Diana, who had no brother or first cousin, was a happy audience to this banter. She regretted the arrival of some people who knew the Lewises, which put a temporary end to their intimacy and informality.

CHAPTER 6

The St Clair sisters, accompanied by Mrs Harcourt, attended the dancing at the Assembly Rooms that evening. Diana was forced to borrow one of Maria's gowns, for a dancing partner's clumsy foot had rendered her jonquil gown in need of repair, and her puce was being laundered. She found Pomona green little more to her taste, though it looked well enough on Maria, with her darker colouring. Henrietta's gowns were no use, for she was shorter than her sisters. And while a hem may easily be taken up, as Mrs Harcourt had observed, the reverse is not the case.

Mrs Harcourt had cautioned the sisters against wearing an excess of jewellery. Henrietta had been unable to resist a necklace of coral and rose quartz, that she had seen in the window of a fashionable jeweller's shop. She had planned to wear it with her rose gown and was nettled by Mrs Harcourt's kindly meant advice.

"You may of course wear it if you wish, my dear, only it is not so much the fashion to be heavily adorned in society at the present time. A married marchioness may wear a tiara and a river of diamonds, but for younger women, it is considered to be conspicuous."

Mrs Harcourt had carefully avoided using the word "vulgar" but her implication was clear. Henrietta felt doubly resentful for this, as well as the inference that she was not au fait with current fashions. Which of course none of the St Clairs were, having been isolated in a small village during the past years.

Maria, who was very conscious of propriety, managed to

calm her sister. "If it is the domain of older women to bedeck themselves, then you may look all the more maidenly unadorned, Henrietta."

This did something to soothe Henrietta's feelings, but Diana's suggestion settled the matter. "Only consider that one of your suitors may be inspired to make you a present of some bauble, by the sight of your bare neck."

Maria frowned at this, but the image of gentleman falling over themselves with gifts of pearls and gemstones was enough to sway Henrietta. "Very well. But I shall wear my coral ring, for I have delicate hands and it becomes them well."

Maria and Diana exchanged a glance at this, unknowing whether to sigh or smile at their middle sister's vanity. She could not be blamed for enjoying herself, Diana reasoned, and it was true that Henrietta was considered one of the best-looking young women in town.

Susannah Lewis greeted her warmly when they met amid the crush of people. She was accompanied by her mother, whom Diana had met and liked, as well as Charles Lewis. This gentleman was introduced to Mrs Harcourt and the elder St Clair sisters. Diana detected that they were favourably impressed by him, though they attempted a polite reserve. Diana was later gratified that while Charles engaged her for two dances, he did not enter his name in the card of either Maria or Henrietta.

The St Clairs had not been fortunate enough to have a dancing master, but Mrs St Clair had schooled them in the steps that she had danced in her younger years. Careful observation and some practice at the Harcourts' house updated this tuition, for the waltz had not been danced in Mrs St Clair's day.

"I am disappointed to learn that you leave us for London," Charles said as they danced the quadrille. "Do you often visit the capital?"

Diana confessed that it would be her first visit. "I do not know what Susannah may have told you, but our fortunes are quite recently reversed. Our family estate was sold after my father's death, but a short time ago we received a legacy from a distant uncle."

She did not think it improper to mention this, for everyone around town was aware of the St Clairs' inheritance. People do not suddenly reappear in society after several years of obscurity without arousing interest. And a large bequest is always news, not to mention the curiosity of the sheep.

Montague Chalmers was amused and intrigued when the Duke of Eastleigh indicated he would attend the dancing in the Assembly Rooms. The Duke had shown no such indication to do so before. Monty bit his tongue when Eastleigh had suggested it, wondering if it related to the recent abandoning of his marriage plans. Perhaps he had decided to cast an eye over the currently available women, to refresh his list?

The Duke did not want to admit to Monty, to himself or to anyone else his true reason for attending. Which was that he wished to catch one more glimpse of the golden-haired young woman, to satisfy himself that he had over-imagined her allure. This at least was what he attempted to convince himself.

In all his thirty-seven years, the Duke of Eastleigh had never found himself seriously distracted by any woman. There had been a brief period of infatuation with a French demi-mondaine, some years older than him, when he had been on the brink of manhood. Since then he had prided himself on being above such sentimentality. His focus had been on his estate and the duties of the duchy.

He was now irritated by the intrusion of this unknown chit into his thoughts. To see her one more time would effect a cure.

Monty perceived that his friend was tense. The Duke stood stiffly at the back of the room, declining to engage in conversation with anyone. He spoke courteously but briefly to each person who approached him, and his dismissal of them was clear.

"You disappoint the ambitious mammas, Eastleigh," Monty remarked. "Doubtless there is much speculation as to your matrimonial intentions, since your expected betrothal has not been announced."

"I cannot imagine why my private affairs should be a matter of public interest," the Duke said, his manner stiff.

"Come now, you can hardly blame them. Marriageable dukes are thin on the ground," Monty joked. "You may as well have entered a tiger's nest by coming here."

"Tigers do not nest," the Duke observed.

Mutual friends approached at that point and suggested retiring to the card room. Monty, who was inordinately fond of cards, joined them with enthusiasm. But the Duke declined.

The moment Monty had gone, he saw her. She was smiling as she turned in a dance step with her partner. The Duke was captivated. She was easily the most beautiful woman in the room. Doubtless she knew it, he thought, as did whatever foolish fop she was dancing with.

The dance moved them closer to where the Duke was standing. He heard her laugh and utter the words: "O Charles!" Her voice was soft and low, and her laughter held an enticing huskiness.

Despite his composure, the Duke felt his loins tightening. Appalled, he reasoned it must be because she was a wanton. Defying convention, to address her partner so familiarly. He did not stop to consider whether the man she was dancing with might have been her cousin or even her betrothed.

All he knew was that as much as he disapproved of her, he could not get her out of his mind.

Diana was whirling around the floor with Charles, laughing

at an irreverent comment he had just made, when she caught sight of a tall, all-too-familiar figure. Once again he stood apart from the crowd, even though he was amid the crush. Impeccably dressed, erect in bearing, and she did not deceive herself to know that he looked directly upon her.

But what an expression! The man was practically glowering at her. What on earth had she done to earn such disapprobation?

Her indignation and embarrassment rising, she could not immediately tear her eyes away from him. Despite the disdain across his features, Diana still observed their perfectly sculpted regularity and the masculine line of his jaw. He should not be so handsome, she thought. His arrogance should detract from it.

But it did not. The next turning of the dance broke their gaze apart and Diana tried to return her attention to Charles. But the happy spell she had been under with him was past. She could only think of dark grey eyes piercing into hers.

"Are you engaged for the next dance, or would you like refreshments?" Charles asked, as the quadrille drew to a close.

Keen to escape the room, Diana owned that she would welcome a change of scene. Charles escorted her to the refreshments and Diana only wished there might be something stronger than orgeat, to steady her nerves.

"There you are!" Susannah came upon them. She wore a gown of palest peach, adored with seed pearls, and her cheeks were flushed. "It is a dreadful crush tonight, is it not? And every gentleman present seems to make a sport of stepping on my feet."

"If it is every gentleman, I suspect that it is your feet that are at fault," Charles told her.

Susannah swatted him with her fan in mock outrage. "How ungallant to make such an accusation! I was told this very evening - and by a Viscount, no less - that I danced with the grace of a swan."

"Seeing that swans do not dance, I wonder at you taking it for a compliment," was her cousin's reply.

Susannah merely laughed and held out her empty glass to Charles, who replaced it with a filled one. "You see now why my cousin remains unmarried, Diana. There is no gentleman in the land so uncouth."

"He has more manners than a duke at any rate," Diana said, in a moment of indiscretion.

Her friend was mystified. "A duke? Do not tell me you have been dancing with a duke!"

"Quite the contrary. I have been glowered at by a duke, and I know not why," Diana told her.

Both Charles and Susannah were intrigued now. "What Duke may this be?" Charles asked, then answered for himself. "It is the Duke of Eastleigh, I presume. For I have heard that he is in town."

"The Duke of Eastleigh! I did not know that you are acquainted with him," Isabella said.

"I am not. I have never met the man. Yet thrice now he has all but scowled at me. And do not think that it is my fancy, or some imagined vanity that he might deign to look upon me. For it is too frequent and too marked for me to be mistaken."

Susannah was thoughtful. "No, if one were to delude oneself out of vanity, it would be to imagine romantic gazes. And it is certainly not that, you say?"

"Indeed not," Diana confirmed. "I have no notion of what I have done to offend him."

"It must be a case of mistaken identity," Susannah said, to which Charles agreed.

"I know little of the man, but I can think of no other explanation. He has a younger cousin also in Bath, quite a tearabout."

Diana said that she had met the Duke's cousin. "My sisters

were quite taken with him, though I found him rather silly. But I am sure that I was every politeness to him."

"That is most likely it, then," Charles said. "Not that you offended his cousin, but that you have designs upon him. He is known to be fiercely protective of his family. He has refused several suitors on behalf of his half-sister. I know, for a friend of mine was one of those whose hopes were dashed. I have not met the lady myself but I hear she is very fine-looking. He will accept nothing less than a Marquess for her, by all accounts."

"What a very hateful man," Susannah said. "If you attempted to reject my suitors, Charles, in the horrid event that you held any such power over me, I should tip my nose at you and abscond to Gretna Green."

Despite everything, Diana could not bring herself to agree that the Duke was hateful. There was something in his intensity, in his solitary nature, that evoked a softer emotion in her. Even with his greater age, rank and wealth, she felt that he was the one at a disadvantage.

CHAPTER 7

Diana visited her mother before leaving for London. With Orchard House, as they had chosen to name it, so close to Bath, it had been possible to pay regular visits home.

After being admitted by Ellen, newly promoted to housekeeper, Diana found her mother in the morning room, poring over a number of papers. She was heartened to see her mother looking better than she could ever remember. The lines of worry had relaxed from Mrs St Clair's face and she had more colour in her cheeks.

Her mother turned as she entered and was similarly reassured by her daughter's appearance. "How well you look, Diana dear. The Bath scene clearly agrees with you. I trust you are all enjoying yourselves?"

"Very much so. Mrs Harcourt has been very kind," Diana said.

"She has always been a very gracious and generous person," her mother agreed. She indicated a large box of papers. "I have recently received this consignment of documents from the estate of Lord Henry. Only think that he wrote an entire volume on the husbandry of the Cotswold Longhorn! It was not published, so far as I can establish, but it contains the most useful information. We may expect three quarters of the ewes to bear twin lambs. And did you know that you may determine the age of a sheep by inspecting its teeth?"

Diana laughed. "I did not expect you to become such a shepherdess, mamma. I had worried that you might be lonely here, but you have an entire flock for family."

Mrs St Clair agreed that she had become quite fond of the Longhorns. "Though from a distance. I leave it to Tom to inspect their teeth."

Jenny, the parlourmaid, brought in refreshments. As Diana poured the tea, her mother questioned her about Bath society. "Your letters are very entertaining, my dear. But tell me more about the people you have met."

A lively discussion followed, though Diana omitted two names. The first was the Duke, who entered her thoughts rather more than she was comfortable with. She had only seen him on three occasions and had never spoken with him. It was an absurd fancy, she supposed. Likely because she had felt a sense of pique at his contemptuous manner. He had definitely glowered at her the last time she had seen him. She was sure she had not imagined it.

The second was Charles Lewis. Diana liked him very much. But once or twice he had looked at her in a way that he did not regard his cousin, and it had disconcerted Diana. She was not yet used to receiving attention from gentlemen and had no wish to commit herself so soon. Charles Lewis would be an excellent match, she had no doubt about that, but she had always imagined that her sisters would marry well before her.

With Mrs St Clair's health so much improved, there was the possibility that she might be able to join her elder daughters in Bath for a short visit. Diana was excited to hear this. "Do you really think so, mamma? The doctor does not object?"

"He is all encouragement. He said a change of scene might well be a tonic, now the weather is more clement. Though I fear I may miss my woolly friends!"

Diana laughed at this, viewing the distant white sheep on the hillside. "They will be well cared for by Tom. We are fortunate to have found such a dedicated shepherd."

"Quite so. It is a shame that he cannot speak, but he understands well. I had thought to have a croft house built at the edge of the wood. Tom's mother is about to welcome her eighth child, and their cottage is already very crowded, even with the eldest girls in service."

Diana considered this an excellent plan. "Do not overtax yourself though, mamma. Let Mr Richards take care of it." Mr Richards, a land agent, had helped the St Clairs with various matters relating to their new property. Mrs St Clair had found him an honest and knowledgeable man and continued to consult him when needed.

Mrs St Clair was also very admiring of the new gowns that Diana had ordered. "You have very good taste, my dear. I confess I was a little uncertain as to the choices your sisters had made. But they are older, and different styles may be more becoming. They are as happy as you, I trust?"

"Very much so. Henrietta is quite deluged with suitors, while Maria is not without invitations. Mrs Harcourt keeps a careful watch for fortune hunters."

Interest from impoverished gentlemen with an eye on the St Clair money had come as an unwelcome surprise to the sisters. They should have expected it, Diana thought. At least with a man like Charles Lewis, rich in his own right, one might be assured that he did not have his eye on a pecuniary prize. Diana was reluctant to reject suitors simply because they suffered less fortunate circumstances, particularly as her own family had suffered lengthy poverty. It was hypocritical, she knew. But she could see the sense in money marrying money.

"If I should marry," she announced to her mother, "it shall only be based on mutual respect and love."

Mrs St Clair hid a smile at this statement. Diana was still of very tender years. "You may consider yourself lucky to be able to choose that basis for marriage. Many women are not spoilt for choice."

"Our father was not a very wealthy man when you married him," Diana pointed out.

"He was not. But while I have never regretted our marriage" - Mrs St Clair's eyes softened as she recalled the handsome, convivial Rainault - "I have felt remorse at the circumstances it forced upon you three. For myself I might easily have borne our poverty, but it has been hardest for Henrietta and Maria."

"If one of us had been a boy, it might have been better," Diana said. A man might earn a living and support his family.

Her mother was unsure. "There would have been the matter of education. I do not know that your father would have wished a son to go into trade, and I do not know what else we might have managed. But for my part I consider myself more than blessed to have three daughters. And your father was no less delighted by your birth than by your sisters'."

The Duke of Eastleigh was to leave Bath. He had ended negotiations with Amberforth with no ill feeling on either side. The Duke's pride might have been affected had Lady Jane shown a preference for another suitor. But even he could feel no resentment at coming second to the Almighty.

Amberforth, aware that his daughter had shown no enthusiasm for Eastleigh or any other suitor, was merely relieved that the Duke was not offended. "It is good of you, sir, to depart with such grace. I hope that you do not find Jane ungrateful. She is - as am I - deeply cognisant of the honour you bestowed on us. But I fear that her preference is for hymns rather than hymeneals."

The Duke gave a rare smile at Amberforth's pun. "It is no dishonour to a family for a daughter to become a Bride of Christ, should that be Lady Jane's choice."

"It may well be." Amberforth gave a sigh. "I do not doubt that it will disappoint her mother, though."

The two men parted friends, with expressions of mutual regret.

Regret was not the emotion the Duke felt as he left Amberforth. Relief, if not elation, might be closer to his true feelings. He dined privately, having given orders for preparations to be made for his return to London the following morning.

The Honourable Frederick, who was back again in Bath, raising a riot with his new stallions, dropped by to farewell his cousin. "I shall see you in London before long. Albemarle and I are arranging a race up the Strand. With Satan and Saul drawing my phaeton, he won't stand a chance, of course."

"That is a wager I would prefer not to make," the Duke said. He was fond of his younger cousin and privately amused at many of his antics. But he judged it wise not to make Frederick aware of this. As the head of the family, a sterner tone was fitting.

"Tanqueray is backing me for twenty guineas," Frederick retorted.

The Duke had been wavering on a matter he had been determined not to waver on. "Those three women with whom I saw you talking at the Assembly Rooms a week or so ago. Who were they?"

His cousin, who had conversed and danced with so many women that season that he could barely distinguish one from another, confessed he had no idea. "Pretty damsels, were they? I'm hopeless with names, I'm afraid. Better with faces than names."

No one could forget such a face, the Duke thought, the image of the golden-haired beauty once again disrupting his serenity. He shared neither this sentiment nor its accompanying vision with Frederick.

"They were three sisters, perhaps?" While not alike, their similarly vulgar dress had linked them.

Frederick wrinkled his brow. it wasn't a brow that did a lot of wrinkling, for he wasn't a great thinker. "You might mean the St Clairs. Though I can't say for certain. They've left Bath, I believe, or one of them has."

"All three are unmarried?" the Duke asked.

This was misunderstood by his cousin. "Oh, you may have no fear along those lines. Given you've waited until well past forty, I see no reason to entangle myself before thirty. A lot of bother, a wife. Might put a stop to the racing. Want gowns and gewjaws above a decent horse. No, that's not for me."

The Duke forbore to mention that he was as yet several years below that ripe age, not above it. Frederick had also failed to answer his question, and the Duke was reluctant to press him further.

Frederick departed, and the Duke considered how he might make further discreet inquiries about the St Clairs. It would be better, he decided, to put them out of his mind.

His plan to return to the capital was interrupted by a letter from an old friend, inviting him to their country home in Sussex. "The river is fairly leaping with trout, for which I know you have a fondness," the letter said.

The Duke, who enjoyed both the eating of trout and the sport of fishing for it, was swayed by this. With no other urgent business pressing him, a sojourn in Sussex seemed very suitable.

CHAPTER 8

The Hollises' house was far beyond what Diana had expected, based on Mary's modest description. It was a very smart townhouse located in an elegant and leafy street overlooking St James's Park. It had also been fitted out with every comfort and convenience, as Diana was to discover.

Mary greeted her joyfully, coming into the hallway herself as the manservant opened the door to admit Diana. "You are here! I trust the journey was as comfortable as can be expected? It is my one regret, that London is so very far from Didmarton."

Diana, who had travelled in a hired post-chaise accompanied by Jenny, assured Mary that the journey had been tranquil. "We were not set upon by highwaymen, though the postilions carried pistols."

"Where did you break the journey? At Reading?" Mary asked.

"No, at Newbury. In a very pleasant inn, that my mother's friend Mrs Harcourt recommended. She has stayed there with her husband en route to London. The linens were clean, and the food very good." In truth the entire journey had been an enormous adventure for Diana. She had never travelled so far, let alone without her mother or sisters. It had also seemed a shocking luxury to hire a post-chaise, but Mrs St Clair had insisted that the stagecoach would not do.

Mary expressed relief at this. "I am sure you must be tired and longing for bed. But you will want supper first. Would you prefer to take it in your room? I will show you there now."

Dismissing a maid who hovered in attendance - "you may return to the kitchen, Fanny, and take Miss St Clair's maid with you, I am sure she will be in need of refreshment" - Mary escorted Diana up the stairs herself.

Diana noted the elegant furnishings as they ascended and commented on these to Mary. "It is all quite beautiful, Mary. You were too modest in your description."

Mary looked embarrassed but pleased. "I own I am very happy with it and consider myself very fortunate. But I forget myself, or rather my husband. I am afraid Matthew dines out late tonight. It is to do with his business, he could not escape it. He sends his every regret at not being here to welcome you. I have told him all about you, and he is very eager to know you."

Whether this was true, or had been said to please his wife, Diana could only guess. But she surmised from her surroundings that Matthew Hollis must be very successful in his business, and by all accounts - or at least Mary's - an excellent husband.

She was shown to a tastefully furnished room where a fire had been laid in the grate, but not lit. "I was unsure as to whether you might wish for a fire, but if you do, Fanny will light it for you," Mary said.

A fire in April was a remarkable luxury. Diana, who did not typically feel the cold, thanked her hostess but assured her that she would not need it.

"I am determined you should have every comfort," Mary said. "Only see this!" She led Diana onto the landing once more and opened a door adjacent to the bedroom. "It is a water closet, quite newly installed. Matthew insisted that we have the latest accommodations. He has even talked of a portable bath shower, through which hot water might be pumped. But you do not wish to hear about plumbing, I am sure! Nor is it a seemly subject to be discussing with a guest. Forgive me."

Diana, laughing, said that there was nothing to forgive. "On the contrary, it is very intriguing. I am unused to any of these novelties."

She inquired as to Mary's son, to be told, as she had expected, that the young fellow was long in bed. "But you will meet him tomorrow," Mary promised, "and I hope he will be on his very best behaviour, so you receive a favourable impression."

"I am sure no child of yours could be anything but angelic," Diana said. "Only remember the rod of iron with which you ruled us in the schoolroom!"

This description was so far from the truth that both women laughed. Mary had been a gentle teacher and much appreciated by all the St Clairs. Her sisters would be amazed, Diana thought, to see Mary now. They likely imagined she resided in some humble cottage, not a house as graceful as this.

Breakfast was served at nine o'clock. Diana, who had woken early, sat by her bedroom window, writing a letter to her mother. London seemed grey at this hour, though the street scene that the window overlooked was lively. Delivery men wheeled carts about, weaving their way past carriages, and an old woman was selling bread and nosegays of flowers from a stall set up on the corner.

Diana had little as yet to write about, but she knew that her mother would be anxious about her long journey. She was at least able to assure Mrs St Clair that she and Jenny had travelled safely, and to pass on her thanks to Mrs Harcourt for suggesting such a comfortable and convenient coaching inn. Deciding she could finish the letter later, after she had met Matthew Hollis and William, she laid down her pen and made some finishing touches to her toilette. Jenny had not travelled so well as she had, so Diana had instructed her not to rise early.

She was not entirely comfortable with having a maid all to herself, though she supposed she ought to get used to it. Even sharing an attendant with her sisters in Bath had seemed a luxury. Diana determined to send Jenny back to Bath if opportunity presented itself.

Matthew Hollis turned out to be a handsome, kind and intelligent gentleman, utterly devoted to Mary, which satisfied Diana. Mary, with her sweet nature, deserved no less. Master William was a cherub with chestnut curls and an astonishingly loud wail when informed that he might not have a second bun, for he had not finished his first. He had been allowed to sit at the breakfast table as a special treat, to meet the new guest. But he was far more interested in the lavish spread than in Diana.

"You will regret your indifference one day, my man," his father told him, ruffling the child's hair. "Your nurse had better take you back upstairs and wash your sticky face and hands. I apologise for my son's lack of manners, Miss St Clair." He was joking, for the child was only a few months past his first birthday, and had no words except "mamma", "ball" and "bun".

"Mary tells me you have recently moved to Bath," Matthew Hollis said.

"We have, or rather to a small village just outside. The legacy that we were fortunate to receive included a flock of sheep. My mother did not think the streets of Bath would accommodate them," Diana explained.

"A flock of sheep! I hope they are not troublesome in upkeep?"

Diana said that they were not. "On the contrary, they are very placid and undemanding animals. They graze on the hillside and drink from a stream and make very few demands on us at all. They are a rare breed, called Cotswold Longhorns."

Matthew Lewis confessed he knew little of farming matters. "It is something I should remedy, for ignorance in any field is to be regretted. But my business sends me to towns and ports, with little leisure to spend in the countryside. I regret it more for Mary's sake than mine, for I am sure she must miss being surrounded by woods and meadows."

Mary assured her husband that she did not long for Arcadia. "The park is more than ample for greenery and trees," she told him. "If this fine weather holds, for I detect no sign of rain, Miss Lewis and I might accompany Nurse on William's morning walk."

Diana welcomed the plan, being keen to see as much of London as soon as possible.

"Very well. If we are ready to leave soon, we may catch the changing of the guard. It is quite a spectacle," Mary said.

Diana enjoyed her time greatly with the Hollises. Their friends were not grand or titled, but they were interesting and diverse people. She was gratified to be spoken to as an equal, not a young and green maiden, though she was several years younger than most of them.

Matthew Hollis had been impressed by Diana's knowledge of business. He did not think it at all unsuitable for a woman to take an interest in investments and shares.

Diana learnt a great deal from the conversations around the Hollises' dinner table, as well as at the homes of people they dined with. This was not solely about business affairs but also on politics, music and art. The Hollises were acquainted with a man who was an upcoming portrait painter, who vowed to paint Diana one day "in the Grecian style."

They visited Montagu House to see the collections of the British Museum, where Diana was much taken with the Egyptian Mummy and the sculptures from the Temple of Apollo. Stuffed birds and dried botanical samples interested her far less.

The issue of the Luddites was much discussed among the Hollis's set, for many were in industry or had links to it. Diana found there was sympathy for the Luddites' plight, if not for their actions in breaking machinery. Rising grain costs and growing unemployment were another concern, and there were fears that the rioting already seen in the east of the country would spread further.

A fortnight after her arrival, Mary broke the news that Matthew must travel to Brighton for some days on business. "But if you are agreeable, he wonders if we might accompany him and make a holiday of it? The sea air is pleasant at this time of year, and there is much to see there."

Diana was agreeable. She had never been to the seaside and Brighton was famous for being a favourite resort of the Prince Regent. There was widespread talk of his extravagances there.

"I should very much love to go. I will write to tell my mother, but I am sure we need not wait for her reply. She has often spoken of Weymouth, which she visited as a child, and wished that we might one day go there. So I am sure that she will not object to my visiting another seaside resort."

Arrangements were rapidly made. Rooms at one of the town's best inns were booked: the party was to include Diana, Mary and Matthew, and William and his nurse. Mary did not plan to take a maid, for the nurse might carry out such small tasks as were required. Like Diana, she had grown up unaccustomed to having a personal attendant and was used to managing many of the affairs that such a person typically took care of. Diana used this as an opportunity to send Jenny back to Bath. There had been very little for Jenny to do in London, and it seemed an extravagance for her to remain there when Mrs St Clair would have greater need of her. Diana also knew that Jenny was courting and must miss her young man.

CHAPTER 9

It could only be Fate that had sent her there, although the Duke was not a man who believed in superstition or predestination. Having spent an agreeable sojourn on his friend's Sussex estate, enjoying much success with the trout, he had taken a trip to Brighton. Strolling along the promenade one morning, appreciating the bracing sea air, he cast his gaze along the shorefront.

He stopped in his tracks, frozen.

There, at the water's edge, hand in hand with some small child, was the young woman from Bath. The sea breezes blew her bonnet back, causing golden strands to fly loose as she raised the infant in the air, laughing.

The Duke felt his heart constrict. In the sunlight, she seemed an angel and he could only gaze at her. All previous notions of her vulgarity dissolved away. He must find out who she was. He wondered at the child: a young brother, perhaps, or a nephew?

He must find out who she was. Frederick had mentioned a family by the name of St Clair but had not been certain.

Summoning his manservant, who was waiting a few paces away, the Duke indicated the figures on the shore. "Establish who that young woman is," he commanded, giving no explanation as to why he sought this knowledge.

He found himself tempted to linger but did not do so. The street would not be a proper place for them to meet, and there was no one who might make appropriate introductions.

Momentarily regretting the propriety demanded by society, the Duke moved on. He cast frequent glances back towards them, half-wishing a wave might sweep over them, allowing him to take the role of rescuer. This led to the vision of a water-drenched gown clinging to a slim form, the fabric translucent over the soft curve of a breast. The reaction he had experienced at the Assembly Rooms came back with even more force, and it was with some difficulty that the Duke managed to continue on his way.

Diana had no awareness that she and William were observed as they frolicked at the water's edge. That morning there had been much excitement during breakfast. The Hollises had received an invitation from Lord Cavendish, the man Matthew was in Brighton to see on business. "Only think that Lord and Lady Cavendish have asked us for lunch! It is a very great honour," Mary had said.

Diana had been pleased for them both. Lady Cavendish was very prominent in society and her name was frequently in the newspapers. A philanthropist and a campaigner for several causes, she was extremely well connected and wealthy in her own right.

But then disaster had struck. William's nurse had been taken ill with a severe stomach complaint and had been in no position to look after him. At such short notice it would have been all but impossible to interview and hire a replacement, and Mary had not been able to countenance leaving him with just anyone.

"But what is the problem?" Diana had said. "I can watch him for you. We shall spend the day at the sea, though I do not think we will get Dipped." It was possible to hire a bathing machine at Brighton and have a "Dipper" push one through the waves. There had been a merry discussion about this at supper. But neither Mary nor Diana had found it an appealing prospect, with the seawater so cold.

Mary had been relieved and grateful for Diana's offer to mind her son, and readily accepted.

This was how Diana had come to be on the beach, sharing William's delight in the waves and collecting shells and sea-smoothed pebbles.

She was happily unaware, as they played, of their dark-haired, distinguished onlooker. William was an entertaining child who had a love of toy boats, which he saw on the pelican lake in St James's Park. Seeing life-sized models on the water thrilled him and he had added the word "bo" to his vocabulary.

"Perhaps you will be a ship's captain one day," Diana told him as they watched a white-sailed vessel on the horizon.

The Duke's manservant completed his quest and returned to the house where his master was staying. He discreetly cleared his throat to alert the Duke to his presence.

"Well, Hawkins?"

"I have investigated the matter, Your Grace. I saw that they returned to the Ship Inn, where I was able to make inquiries. I am informed that the young woman with a small boy is a Mrs Hollis of St James's Park, London. She is staying here with her husband, a Mr Matthew Hollis. He is in business, some form of imports and exports…"

The Duke cut him off with a wave of his hand. He had heard enough. "Thank you, Hawkins. That is more than sufficient."

He had not been prepared for the bitter wave of disappointment that swept him. He had never formulated any intentions towards the young woman. But now that no intentions could be formulated, the Duke felt oddly bereft.

What had come over him? Did he grow sentimental with his increasing years? What was she, after all? Merely a female with hair an attractive shade of gold and arresting grey eyes. An unusual silver grey, he recalled. And a voice that was low and sweet, with a laugh that…

He checked himself. There was no point in further

contemplation. The woman was married and beyond reach.

For the first time he questioned the wisdom of having left his own marriage plans so late. She would not be the only woman to have exited the market. Unless he fancied some green chit freshly entered into society, which he did not.

A young widow might be more his lot. A woman who had borne a child might be a surer bet to produce an heir for Eastleigh.

Trying to banish such thoughts from his mind, the Duke turned his attention to more pressing matters. One of these was Honoria Cavendish's damnable ball on Friday night. He supposed he had better attend the rout. He had great regard for both the Cavendishes. Honoria Cavendish wouldn't be affronted if he didn't attend, but he would be in her good favour if he did.

The Hollises returned later that afternoon. Mary was full of enthusiasm for Cavendish House and its owners. "Lady Cavendish is very gracious. I confess I was apprehensive to meet her, for it is always said that she has a great intellect. But she does not condescend. She is very interesting on so many different subjects. Yet that is not the most exciting thing that I have to tell you. For she is to give a ball in a few days, and we are all invited! You as well, Diana."

"But how could she invite me? I have no acquaintance with her," Diana said.

"I spoke of you to her, for she asked about our plans in Brighton. I mentioned that we were travelling with a friend, and she regretted that she had not known, or would have included you in the lunch invitation."

Diana questioned what sort of a ball it would be and what kind of people would be there. Mary did not know.

"Cavendish House is amply sized and there is a large ballroom there, so there may be very many. I cannot say. Only it is fortunate that we have our best gowns with us, for otherwise I do not know what we should do," Mary said.

Her husband, who had been occupying himself with their son, saw no issue in this. "We should simply send for your gowns. Or purchase new ones."

How like a man to consider the complex matter of a woman's wardrobe so trivial. Mary and Diana exchanged a glance. Later, when they were alone, Mary expressed more anxiety. "We must engage a maid as well. If only I had brought Fanny! And a carriage must be arranged. You may wonder at my being so flustered. But you have seen how simply we live in London. We do not dine with grand people, and I am anxious that we should not appear - well, that we should not embarrass Lady Cavendish in any way."

Diana reassured Mary that this would not be the case. "Your father was a gentleman, Mary, as was mine. Your husband is as well." Matthew Hollis, like the Reverend Elford, had been a younger son, necessitating a profession. Diana knew that the Church was considered a more gentlemanly profession than trade, though she privately thought this foolish. "But even if they were not gentlemen, we are invited as guests. Lady Cavendish must accept us as we are."

Mary agreed that her worries were likely misplaced. "But I am anxious that I do not expose myself, for Lord Cavendish is a very important client of Matthew's."

"I do not see how you could do anything but delight everyone, Mary dear. Now let us determine what we will wear, and if we will need to employ a seamstress for any small repairs. For my needlework has never satisfied my mamma, and I fear I will do more harm than good if I attempt any mending."

CHAPTER 10

Diana was impressed as their carriage drove up to the entrance of Cavendish House. She had been to a couple of private balls in Bath, but none had been such a grand affair as this promised to be. There were liveried footmen in attendance outside, urns of flowers positioned up the steps, and she glimpsed vast chandeliers lighting up the hallway.

Diana had chosen to wear her favourite gown: one of the ones she had ordered for herself in Bath, with Mrs Harcourt's assistance. In white silk with a silver thread, it had been an expensive garment. She had compromised by choosing only two more gowns, rather than three, and those as inexpensive as possible. Mrs Harcourt had approved all of these selections, knowing what would pass muster and what would not.

Now, with her hair becomingly arranged by the deft fingers of the lady's maid that Mary had engaged, Diana felt fully fit to appear in any society.

And what society it was! Lady Cavendish, being well-connected and well-respected, could count on her friends travelling down from London for her balls and parties. They were an eclectic mix, ranging from marquises to wealthy merchants. The Cavendishes were great proponents of progress and social democracy, and Lady Cavendish was even said by some to be a radical.

Diana, who knew no one there, made an effort to remember all the people she was introduced to. Her hostess, at least, was unforgettable. Lady Cavendish wore a magnificent gown of crimson tulle embroidered with gold. A tiara of rubies or garnets crowned her already impressive height.

Diana curtseyed as she was introduced to Lady Cavendish,

lowering her gaze. She did not expect her hostess to address her beyond a polite nod, for there were many guests waiting to pay their respects.

She was startled when that lady did speak to her, in a deep and resonant voice. "St Clair? I have heard of the family. Your great-uncle - or perhaps great-great uncle, for you seem very young - was a notorious rogue."

Diana had absolutely no response to this other than: "yes, my lady."

Honoria Cavendish laughed. "I don't doubt the tales of Rainault's exploits have been well buried along with him."

Diana felt horrified. "Rainault St Clair was my father, my lady."

Lady Cavendish looked all the more amused. "Rainault the Rogue died more than thirty years ago. You may comfort yourself that it was not the same gentleman, my dear."

Bewildered, Diana thanked her once again. Her hostess was regarding her with interest.

"We will speak later. For now, enjoy yourself. I have invited a good number of young people, for a gathering of only the elderly is a dreary affair, is it not?"

She moved on and Diana rejoined the Hollises who had overheard the exchange. "Heavens, how well you composed yourself, Diana dear. I should not have known how to react if I thought my father were branded a rogue!" Mary said.

The prospect of anyone maligning the genteel Reverend Elford was so absurd that Diana had to suppress laughter. She was still dazed from the exchange.

The early part of the evening was indeed wonderfully enjoyable for Diana. There were enough young people to fill the dance floor, and she found herself in continuous demand as a dancing partner. Gentleman after gentleman filled her card and she danced until her feet ached.

The men she met at the Cavendish ball were in general

more interesting than those she had met in Bath, save perhaps for Charles Lewis. Diana was happy to converse and flirt. Her gaiety attracted admirers like moths to a flame: she was easily the most popular young woman in the room, though she was unaware of this.

Such was Diana's absorption in the dancing and conversation that she was also unaware of the arrival of a figure who stood, unsmiling, in a position that overlooked the dance floor.

Of all the people the Duke of Eastleigh had expected to encounter at the Cavendishes' rout, it was not this disturbing young woman. How she had come to be there he had little idea. Honoria had been typically catholic in her choice of guests.

Now, once again observing the golden-haired woman, he found himself enraged by what he perceived to be her coquettish display. He lacked the self-awareness to attribute his ire to its true cause: a violent jealousy. For this was an emotion entirely new to the Duke.

Torn between gazing upon her and unable to bear the sight of her flirtatious attentions to other men, the Duke wavered. Then he turned on his heel and strode out.

"Eastleigh!" a friend greeted him but the Duke did not even hear. He went to a room set aside for cards, taking a goblet from a tray-bearing servant, and stood by the wall, his mood thunderous.

"Eastleigh is in a foul humour tonight," another person remarked.

"Word has it that Amberforth's girl rejected him."

"An *alliance convenable*, surely? Not a grand passion," the first observer said. "All the more so at his age."

"Who can say? Bidforth challenged Grevesby's eldest for the Tanqueray girl, and both were past forty, or thereabouts."

None of this conversation carried to the ears of the Duke, who was incensed enough by his own thoughts. Damn the woman. Carrying on like a libidinous debutante. The incongruity of this phrase did not strike him. He knew only that he was furious and in no mood for company.

Diana, had still not sighted the Duke and had no idea that he was among Lady Cavendish's guests. Let alone that he had once again stood and glowered at her. So her pleasure in the evening was entirely uninhibited, until the fateful moment that her latest partner escorted her to the refreshment room.

There, the not uncommon combination of someone's trailing hem, another's clumsy foot and the general crush of the crowd sent her careering into a hard and unyielding form.

Diana looked up and wished the world might end.

She had collided with the Duke of Eastleigh.

She had not stood this near to him before and he was all the more devastatingly attractive close up. And she had nearly knocked him off balance. No wonder he looked incandescent with rage.

The crowd around them had rapidly ebbed away, seeing the ire on the Duke's face.

Diana, though the trip was far from her fault, for she had been shoved by some unknown person, attempted to apologise. "My lord - Your Grace - I beg your pardon..." she was flustered, knowing not what to say or how to address him.

The Duke, who was having to exert an inordinate amount of self-control due to her proximity, silenced her. "I am uninterested in anything you have to say, madam." His contemptuous emphasis on the word "madam" was clear.

"I am sorry, I did not..." Diana began again, and once again he interrupted her.

"I have observed your behaviour this evening. I am thus unsurprised that after flinging yourself at half the gentleman in the room, you - no doubt drunkenly - fling yourself at yet another victim."

Diana gasped in bewilderment. What could he mean by such an attack? Thoughts and questions raced through her mind: had her conduct been reproachable? Had she made a spectacle of herself?

The Duke continued. "Mores may be different among the younger people of today, but for a married woman to comport yourself as you do is a disgrace. I can only pity your husband and child, that you humiliate yourself and dishonour your family in this fashion." His voice was low and grave yet held the emotion of deep anger.

Despite her shock, Diana began to realise that some hideous error had been made. The Duke clearly mistook her for some other woman. She did not know how this mix up had occurred, nor why he had chosen to berate her in this manner. She was mortified both for herself and for him.

With no further words, the Duke of Eastleigh turned sharply from her and departed.

Diana stood there for several moments in great distress. She was uncertain what to do. She saw that a few curious eyes were upon her. They had not been close enough to overhear, but doubtless wondered at the abruptness of the Duke's departure.

Her greatest desire was to flee and to be as far away as possible. But there were Mary and Matthew to consider. She must compose herself and endure the rest of the evening as though nothing had happened.

As the night progressed the wine had flowed, and if there were less gaiety in her manner than before, her dancing partners either did not notice or attributed it to fatigue.

Only Mary remarked on a change in her friend. "Are you quite well, dear? I worry that you exhaust yourself with all the dancing. If you should wish to retire, Matthew can call for the carriage."

Diana reassured her that everything was fine. "But you are right in that I have danced more than I am used to. I will sit out the next ones."

This was worse, for doing so gave Diana more time to brood. Only the approach of her hostess caused her to abandon her tormented thoughts.

Taking a seat and indicating for Diana - who had risen - to do the same, Lady Cavendish asked how she fared. "You are enjoying yourself, Miss St Clair? The gentlemen do not tread on your toes?"

As gallingly close as this was to her recent humiliation, Diana managed a smile. "I do not know when I have enjoyed myself so much, my lady." This at least was true for the first half of the evening.

"I am glad to hear it. My own dancing days are long past, but as a girl I was very fond of it. You are staying in Brighton, are you not?"

Diana said that she was.

"Then I hope very much that you will visit us again during your stay."

Unsure as to how serious an invitation this was, or whether mere civility, Diana thanked Lady Cavendish. "I would be honoured."

"We shall arrange it. The almanack augurs rain and high winds tomorrow. It will not be a day to spend on the seafront. Why don't you come for tea?"

"I would be delighted, my lady. Only I am staying with friends, and do not know what their plans may be. I hope it does not offend you if I beg leave to check with them first?"

This did not at all offend Lady Cavendish, who looked amused. "By all means, my dear."

Mary had no fixed plans and it was thus arranged that a carriage would be sent for Diana the next afternoon. Both women wondered at the summons from so important a personage. It did something to assuage Diana's distress over her earlier humiliation.

CHAPTER 11

Diana little knew what to expect when she descended from the carriage at Cavendish House. She and Mary had puzzled over it but were none the wiser as to why Lady Cavendish had singled her out.

There were no other guests: it was only Lady Cavendish and herself to whom the maid brought tea. Lady Cavendish poured out, encouraging Diana to partake of the accompanying tray of delicacies.

"Your father was the last of the St Clairs, was he not? Of the male line?" Lady Cavendish asked.

"Yes, my lady. There is a branch of the family that moved overseas many years ago, but we have no present contact with them," Diana said.

Lady Cavendish continued to question her. "The St Clair estate is in Gloucestershire, I believe?"

"It is, or rather, it was. The Hall was sold after my father's death, and we moved to a village called Didmarton. It was there that I made the acquaintance of Mrs Matthew Hollis."

Lady Cavendish nodded. "An intelligent woman. I was much impressed by her when we first met the other day. My husband regards Mr Hollis as one of the most astute young men of his generation."

Diana glowed on her friends' behalf at this praise. "It is kind of you to say so, my lady."

"It is only the truth. Doubtless he will be awarded a baronetcy one day. Though I wonder at the sense of bestowing new titles at all. There is some argument to be made for abolishing such distinctions in society. The rise of men like Mr Hollis may be considered evidence of the irrelevancy of rank in these modern times. You find my views radical, no doubt?"

"Not at all, my lady."

Diana meant no barb by including the polite term of address but Lady Cavendish took it as such and gave a deep chuckle. "Let us only wait until the industrialists are kings of the castles and the nobility retire to cottages on their former estates. For all across England, the great houses are being bought, one by one, by those able to afford their upkeep."

Diana was reminded of Mrs Harcourt's comments, though she did not think that lady had intended them so seriously as Lady Cavendish did. She merely replied: "indeed" as politely as possible.

"At any rate, you would do well to marry one of these clever young men yourself, when you have a mind to marry," Lady Cavendish continued. "How old are you?" Not an age at which you need be coy about your years, I warrant."

Diana smiled. "Not yet. I am seventeen, my lady."

Lady Cavendish studied her. "It is not that you look any older, but your manner is beyond your years. I expect you are curious as to why I have asked you here today."

"It was very kind of you to ask me," Diana said, unsure as to how else to answer.

"Not at all. It was entirely out of self-interest. You have an excellent voice, well-modulated and pleasing to the ear, you are intelligent, and properly educated. Such a combination is not common. I have observed how very shrill the voices of young women are these days."

Diana murmured "thank you", wondering if she were properly modulating the phrase.

"My eyesight is not what it was. It is for this reason that I require someone who can read to me. Miss Anne Havisham, my usual companion, has an excellent voice. But she is presently attending to a sick relative in the north of the country. I wonder if you would consider taking her place in the interim?

I cannot say whether it will be for a week or a twelvemonth, but from Anne's most recent letter, her relative appears to be recovering more quickly than anticipated."

This was an unexpected proposal! Diana chose her words with care. "It is a great compliment you pay me, my lady. I would be more than delighted if I could be of use to you. But I am not presently in need of paid employment. Forgive me if I have created such an impression. For my family recently came into an inheritance that has allowed us a very comfortable living situation."

Lady Cavendish was unperturbed. "Then you may come as my guest. I have quite set my mind on the idea, though I do not go so far as to press the King's shilling upon you."

This was said in deliberate jest, and Diana smiled once again. "If you would permit me to write to my mother, I am confident that she will not refuse."

"Very well. You imagine it will be dull, I don't doubt, reading to an old woman. But we will ensure there is entertainment for you here. And I am hopeful that you will find my reading materials of some interest."

Mary Hollis marvelled at Diana's account of her afternoon with Lady Cavendish, after she rejoined them at the inn in Brighton.

"It is certainly very flattering, though I do not know if that is quite the right term," Mary said. "I am sure that it would not be improper to accept." She turned to her husband, who was studying the shipping column in that day's newspaper. "What do you think, Matthew."

Matthew looked up from his paper. "I think the only question is whether Miss St Clair wishes to accept," he said.

"Do you, Diana?" Mary asked.

"I own I am curious. She is very fascinating and knowledgeable," Diana said.

"She is forthright in her views, certainly," Matthew observed.

Mary was still considering the propriety of the matter. It was difficult to define. There was nothing improper in taking the position of a companion: indeed it was one of the few routes open to poorer gentlewomen, if they did not wish to be governesses. But Diana's family was wealthy, and the St Clairs had no connection with Lady Cavendish.

"She is quite a singular woman," Mary mused. "Some might say eccentric. Though she is very highly regarded nonetheless. I think that it may be an irregular situation, but a lady of her position may set her own rules of conduct. After all, she is the granddaughter of a duke."

Diana could not prevent a movement of her features at this term. It evoked a dreadful memory she was trying to forget. She failed to hide her reaction from the eagle-eyed Mary.

"Something is wrong, Diana dear?"

"It is nothing," Diana assured her.

When a person acknowledges a thing as being nothing, then it is very clearly something. Such was Mary's interpretation of her friend's denial.

"You are troubled on account of Lady Cavendish's offer?"

"No, it is not that at all," Diana said. This naturally confirmed that something did weigh upon her mind, and Mary pressed her to reveal it.

With reluctance, Diana did so. "It is a curious and upsetting business, and I did not wish to trouble you with it. But I am lately wondering if you may be in some way implicated, so perhaps it is right that I tell it."

With some pain, she related her interview with the Duke of Eastleigh. She was not sure if it could fairly be described as an interview, for the word suggested an exchange of communication, and there had been few words allowed from her side. "So you see, Mary, from his mention of my supposed husband and child, I have wondered if our identities had become confused."

Mary, increasingly indignant on Diana's behalf as she heard the tale, agreed this was possible. "But it in no way justified such an attack! Were I to have danced with every man in the room, and tapped each one archly with my fan, I should not expect some other guest to censure me in such a fashion, should I, Matthew?"

"I should greatly like to see you tap each gentlemen archly with your fan, Mary. I imagine it would be a highly amusing spectacle," was her husband's only comment.

"I would certainly have swatted the Duke on his noble nose, for such an unwarranted attack. To be spoken to thus by a man who was surely a complete stranger! For you had never met him, had you, Diana?"

Diana said that she had not. "He was in Bath when I was there, and I was introduced to his cousin." She found herself telling Mary about the strange and angry glares she had received from the Duke of Eastleigh in that town.

Mary was as mystified as she was outraged. "What can he mean by such conduct? It is beyond the pale."

Matthew chuckled. "I should think it is blindingly obvious what he means by it."

"What can you mean?" Mary asked.

"I wonder you find his behaviour so difficult to interpret, given your usual intuition. But I imagine it will all come out in the wash, or whatever the expression is. For he must discover Miss St Clair's true identity in the end."

CHAPTER 12

The Duke of Eastleigh had left Cavendish House shortly after his encounter with Diana. The whole affair had tormented him since.

He knew in his heart he had acted badly, for the conduct of another man's wife was not his business.

Yet he remained enraged.

Who was she, to flaunt her beauty and her charms so wantonly? And to every male in the room, save himself.

This last was the sharpest needle, though the Duke did not acknowledge it.

He paid a visit to Lady Cavendish before leaving Sussex for London. She was in the room that she described as her office, engaged in correspondence.

"Good afternoon, Eastleigh. You will forgive me if I finish dictating this letter. It needs to go with the evening post."

Lady Cavendish's deep tones rung out as her secretary scrambled to take down the final message and customary salutations. "That should suffice, Carruthers. Have Lord Cavendish frank it and ensure that it is taken on time."

Her attention returned to the Duke. Honoria Cavendish always regarded the Duke of Eastleigh as having had the good fortune of an intelligent and well educated mother. Fanny Marchmont, later Beresford, had been a close friend of Honoria's in girlhood. Tutored alongside her brothers, Fanny had been as educated and as knowledgeable as any man.

The sons of such women neither feared nor resented intellect in other women, Honoria had found. It had been a deciding factor in her acceptance of her own husband's proposal. The late Dowager Lady Cavendish had been a formidable woman who had terrified several prospective daughters-in-law into retreat.

Not so Honoria. She had seen a woman whom she might mutually respect and had accordingly deigned to marry her son.

"You come upon me in some disarray, Eastleigh," Lady Cavendish said, turning at last to the Duke. She signalled to a hovering servant. "I doubt tea is much in your line. What will you take? Claret? A brandy?"

The Duke chose brandy and at Lady Cavendish's nod, the servant departed to fetch the decanter.

"With Anne Havisham still away, I have struggled to read the material I need to. It is a blight of old age, this fading vision. But I have managed to engage a new reader, whom I am hopeful will join me shortly. The St Clair girl, whom you may remember at my ball the other night, has agreed to fill the role temporarily."

It was not a name that held a happy resonance for the Duke. "The St Clair girl?"

"You remember. The blonde young woman - quite exquisite looking - who was in so much demand on the dance floor."

The Duke of Eastleigh frowned. He could not think of any blonde woman who matched this description except a particular one he was endeavouring to forget. "I do not recall a Miss St Clair," he said.

"In white silk, with the silver thread. A Parisian model, that gown. Albeit you gentlemen never notice such details. I wonder you did not dance with her yourself, Eastleigh, though you would have had to wait your turn."

There was a coldness in the air. The Duke felt his words suspended. "The blonde woman on the dance floor was a Mrs Hollis, surely?"

Lady Cavendish looked mildly amused. "I hardly think so.

Mrs Hollis may have danced, but she is a brunette. Miss St Clair is a friend of Mrs Hollis. She is staying with Mrs Hollis and her husband in Brighton."

The Duke was having some difficulty articulating his words. "Do you mean that the blonde woman on the dance floor was not a married woman? Quite definitely not married, with a child?"

"I should think not, unless you have evidence to suppose so. The Hollises have a young son."

The Duke stood up abruptly. "I must depart."

"Depart? But you have only just come!"

The servant entered with the decanter at this point, causing even more confusion.

"At least take a glass before you go," Honoria Cavendish urged. "You seem on edge. Steady your nerves."

The Duke took a large draught, hardly knowing what he was drinking, and felt the fiery liquid burn his throat. He scarcely avoided choking. The magnitude of his error was becoming more apparent by the minute.

Not only had he behaved with outrageous rudeness to a total stranger, but his censure had been entirely misplaced.

He remembered the pain and bewilderment in her eyes. If only she had protested more strongly, defied him, even laughed at him. But she had endured his diatribe with composure and sought no redress.

He knew he must apologise, and beg her forgiveness, but how?

Once back at his house in London, the Duke began letter after letter but could not find any appropriate words for such a situation. He had considered calling on her in Brighton before his return to the capital, but his nerve failed.

He was anxious to undo the wrong he had done her. He was also concerned to redeem his good name and reputation. He had always prided himself on his civility and courtesy, and the *noblesse oblige* motto of the Beresford family.

What hubris! How hollow his pride had been.

In his club he suffered further discomfort on hearing the St Clair family discussed by a couple of members. He missed the origins of the discussion, but not the family name.

"The St Clairs? Harrogate's heirs, aren't they?"

"Not Harrogate of the Herd? Didn't have a bean to his name, surely."

"Quite the opposite. A very pretty packet for St Clair's widow, and God knows she could have done with it."

"What of the famous flock? Sheared and on the spit?"

"Left to her as well, I don't know what use they might have been. Some rummy breed old Harry was hung up on. Cotswold Curlies or Banbury Bleaters. I dare say it's all the same as a leg of roast mutton."

The two gentlemen moved on to the dining room, where both were delighted to find shoulder of spring lamb on that day's menu.

It would have to be in person, the Duke decided. There was no way to articulate it in written form. Or no way that he could find.

Mrs St Clair wrote to say that she had no objection and every happiness for Diana to stay with Lord and Lady Cavendish. In truth she was privately relieved that Diana would not immediately be returning to Bath and the society of her sisters. For though she missed her youngest daughter, she was troubled by the influence her elder daughters might have upon her.

Wealth had not improved Maria and Henrietta. This was the reluctant conclusion that Mrs St Clair had been forced to draw when she arrived in Bath. Her health was much improved and Jocasta Harcourt was more than delighted to welcome her friend.

"Do not trouble to arrange private lodgings, for we have more than enough room," she had urged.

Grateful to be spared the task of setting up a new household, Catherine St Clair had accepted her friend's kind offer.

Now, as she watched her daughters across the floor of the Assembly Rooms, she felt uneasy. Maria was become even more haughty, and Henrietta vainer and more flirtatious. Her greatest concern was that other people might regard them unfavourably.

She raised the issue with Jocasta Harcourt. They had been friends for many years, and Mrs St Clair felt able to speak her mind.

"I do not know if I have exercised the wisest judgment, being so liberal with Maria and Henrietta. They are unused to money and position," Mrs St Clair said.

Jocasta Harcourt understood her friend's concerns but sought to allay them. "I dare say it has gone to their heads by some small measure, but they have birth and breeding. People do not look upon them with disfavour. Besides, I do not think either will remain unattached for long."

Henrietta had already received two proposals, neither of which she had cared to accept. She was aiming for high rank if not royalty, though her mother feared she over-reached.

Mrs St Clair was glad to make the acquaintance of the Lewis family and found Susannah to be a charming girl.

"I was sorry to learn that Diana will not be returning immediately to Bath," Miss Lewis said, on being introduced to Mrs St Clair. "But what a wonderful opportunity for her, to be welcomed into the society of Lady Cavendish. She has written to me about it, and I am very glad for her."

"It is indeed an honour for her," Mrs St Clair replied.

"Though she is much missed here," Susannah added. "My cousin and I have been planning a picnic on Claverton Down, to which you are all very welcome. There is a very scenic folly there."

Mrs St Clair had also been introduced to Charles Lewis, and soon guessed that he harboured a fondness for her youngest daughter. She would not have objected to such a match but thought it wiser for Diana not to marry too young. It was better all round if her elder daughters found husbands first.

"Only think!" A flushed and excited Henrietta had returned to the party. "Viscount Marlborough has invited us to go driving with him in the park tomorrow, should the weather be fine. Which it must be. I defy a single cloud to mar the sky."

She fanned herself with yet another new purchase, this one of blush silk and lace embroidered with seed pearls. It was an expensive item, Mrs St Clair observed, but she had to admit it became Henrietta's complexion well.

"I only hope you have more influence over the weather than King Canute had with the tide, my dear," was her mother's response.

CHAPTER 13

Diana enjoyed herself very much during her first week at Cavendish House. Far from being burdensome, she found reading aloud to Lady Cavendish a joy. All the more so because most of the material was interesting and even controversial. Much of it, including a proposed bill on divorce law reform, was not reading matter that would have been permitted to her in other circumstances.

Lady Cavendish was either oblivious to this or did not share society's concern regarding the protection of tender ears.

The topic of the Ponsonby marriage even arose, for that scorned gentleman now sought a dissolution of his marriage.

"He should be granted it, of course. But it is entirely the result of his own folly," was Lady Cavendish's view. "A ten year difference in age may be of no consequence, twenty is highly questionable, and thirty should not even be permitted, by the Church or by Parliament."

"I suppose the lady in question had little choice about accepting him?" Diana said.

This suggestion was vehemently dismissed. "Pah! She was a scheming minx. But she was misled as to the level of his vigour or misjudged it. She ought to have known, for Ponsonby's father lived until his eighties. Were her goal a wealthy widowhood, and I can only assume that it was, she would have done better to have dangled for one of his vintage."

Diana was also present whenever Lady Cavendish received guests. She had expected to have been dismissed, but it was quite the opposite. Lady Cavendish was keen to include her - even to exhibit her - as a form of protégée.

One cloud hung over Diana. This was the anticipation that

she would have to face the Duke of Eastleigh again. He was one of the Cavendishes' friends and there had been more than one mention of him. Diana did not know whether he had yet learnt of his mistake. Her greatest dread was that he would turn up at Cavendish House one day, find her there, and berate her a second time. At which point she would have to correct him as to her identity, increasing their mutual mortification.

Or perhaps she overthought it. Perhaps she was actually of very little consequence to a duke, and he had forgotten his outburst just as he might forget an irritable word to a servant who had misstepped.

Diana was by now confident that there had been nothing untoward in her behaviour at the ball. For surely Lady Cavendish would not have welcomed her into her home if there had been?

The fateful day arrived on a Friday, eight days since Diana's arrival. It had been a wet morning, and Lady Cavendish was out visiting friends. She had insisted that Diana remain behind and enjoy a few hours of leisure - "for I have made more than enough demands on you as it is, my dear".

Diana sat in the parlour writing a letter to Susannah Lewis. She had longed to confide in her about the Duke but shrank from memorialising the incident in ink.

Just as she laid down her pen, gazing out of the window at the grey skies and wet lawns, one of the servants appeared at the door to announce His Grace the Duke of Eastleigh.

Diana felt faint. "Lady Cavendish is not at home," she said.

"His Grace requests an audience with you, madam."

Composing herself as best she could, Diana stood and curtseyed as the Duke entered the room. She murmured "Your Grace" barely daring to look at him.

"Please do not rise, be seated," he said.

Diana did so and waited.

The Duke was silent for a few agonising seconds, then speech burst from him. "It is impossible to find the words to express my deep and sincere apology to you for my conduct at our last meeting. I offer no defence or justification of my behaviour or the calumnies I cast at you. Only know that I have agonised over it ever since, even before I discovered how fatally mistaken I was regarding your identity. My insults to you were inexcusable. I struggle to know what reparations I can make or how I may beg your forgiveness."

How grave he looked! Diana had not seen such an expression on his features before. At all other times he had looked stern or angered.

"You did not insult me, sir, for I realised soon after you began speaking that your words could not be intended for me," she said. "As such there is nothing to forgive."

"You are more than gracious to say so, and it is far more than I deserve." The Duke's tense air of formality wavered. His tone became more urgent, as he spoke with a passionate sincerity. "I have begun a dozen letters to you, Miss St Clair, yet each attempt seemed feebler than the last. Had I known who you were, had we only been introduced in Bath..." he broke off, gazing at her.

Diana, recalling his manner in Bath, and the deep distress and anxiety she had suffered ever since the Cavendishes' ball, could not help a spark of indignation. "I only wonder, sir, that you should speak to any woman such, with whom you were so little acquainted." Even as she spoke she regretted the words and wished she had held her tongue. She had doubtless angered him all over again.

But the Duke's countenance showed only contrition. "Your chastisement is no less than I deserve."

The sorrow on his features melted away the last trace of Diana's ill feeling. She felt only compassion for him, that such a noble and distinguished man felt himself so abased, and by his own conduct.

Hardly knowing what she did, she extended her hand. "Though we are still not formally introduced, I hope that we may part on friendly terms."

She was unprepared for the jolt that ran through her when he took her hand, knelt, and kissed it.

In that moment the Duke of Eastleigh knew only two things.

That this woman, despite her youth and vastly lower social rank, was his equal.

And that he was in love with her.

He wanted nothing more than to take her in his arms and continue to beseech her forgiveness, while begging her to become his wife.

So this is it, the Duke thought. This emotion that he had always scorned in others and thought himself above - or at least incapable of - had overtaken him in the worst possible circumstances.

For he had made a fool of himself, and this girl, whatever her grace in absolving him, must surely hate him.

Regarding the perfection of her features, the beauty of her silvery eyes and the grace and intelligence that shone through them, he had never felt less worthy.

He had an urge to declare himself then and there. To secure her promise and make her his before any other man might do so. He then feared that her heart may already be given to another. She may even be betrothed, or near such a state.

The girl before him could not read the turmoil that was going through his mind. Vainly the Duke sought a reason to prolong the conversation, to find a way that he might ensure that this was not their last meeting.

The words that came were not the words the Duke - or any suitor - would have chosen, had he more time to compose himself.

"I understand that your family keeps a breed of rare sheep?"

The change of topic was so abrupt and so incongruous with everything that had gone before that Diana merely gaped. The Duke was looking at her expectantly.

She did her best to recover herself. "That is so, sir. We are not farmers, but they were part of a bequest to my mother."

He nodded. "There are several rare breeds on my estate in Oxfordshire. I would be honoured if your mother and you would wish to pay a visit and" - he paused, searching for words - "share knowledge of their husbandry."

A duke was asking her to his home to look at sheep. Diana might have laughed were it not for the sincerity in his expression. She guessed that he was trying to do her the honour of showing her that he considered her family fit guests for his home.

"I am sure we would be very honoured by such an invitation, sir." How else could she respond? It must be the kind of invitation made for courtesy's sake only, to be forgotten and never spoken of again after the Duke's departure.

Even as she thought this, she found herself wishing that she might see his estate and see more of him. Was that relief on his features? He was relieved, most likely, that their interview was now at an end.

"That is good. I will make arrangements forthwith," the Duke said. He took his leave with all graciousness.

Diana sat back at the writing desk but was unable to pen a single word. Instead she gazed out once again at the rain-swept gardens, listening to the gravel crackle under the wheels of his departing carriage, until she heard it no more.

When Lady Cavendish returned, Diana told her of the Duke's visit and his unusual invitation. She did not mention any part of their earlier conversation. That entire sorry incident was not something she ever wished to relive.

"He suggested you visit Eastleigh to look at his sheep?"

"Yes." Put so bluntly, it did seem a very unusual invitation. Diana could not explain that she believed it to be his attempt to make amends, since Lady Cavendish was not aware there were any amends to make.

Honoria Cavendish, not sharing Diana's naiveté nor her modesty, interpreted the invitation in quite a different light. She did not approve. What could Eastleigh be thinking, to come to her house and make advances to her guest in her absence? For an advance was undoubtedly what this was.

"Do you wish to visit Eastleigh?" she asked.

Diana hesitated. "I think so, my lady." For she found she very much wanted to, though she was not sure why. The Duke disturbed her. He haunted her thoughts.

And despite everything, despite his disapproval of her and his rudeness to her and his general high-handedness, she felt an odd compassion for him.

CHAPTER 14

Honoria Cavendish made arrangements to call on the Duke of Eastleigh during her next trip to London, which took place just over a week later. Both she and Lord Cavendish had matters of business to attend to in the capital and planned to stay there for some weeks. Diana was to accompany them.

"Should you wish, you might visit your friend Mrs Hollis while we are in town, or any other friends you have there," Lady Cavendish said. She did not want the girl to know of her planned interview with Eastleigh. She intended to talk some sense into the man.

They travelled to London in the Cavendishes' coach, the four seats accommodating Lord and Lady Cavendish, Diana, and Lady Cavendish's maid. Lord Cavendish's man and other servants, along with most of the luggage, had left by stagecoach on the previous day.

Diana was excited to be travelling to London again. It was a distance of some fifty miles, and by setting off early and taking only an hour for lunch with one change of horses, the party was able to arrive in Mayfair by late afternoon.

The Cavendishes' London house was on a far grander scale than the Hollises', but Diana had expected no less. It was situated in Grosvenor Square, and Diana's room overlooked the elegant gardens.

"I expect we shall be made very busy now we are in town," Lady Cavendish said, and news of her arrival there soon brought a stream of visitors, calling cards and invitations.

For all she enjoyed the whirl of social activity, Diana missed the intimacy of the Hollises' quieter dinners and humbler friends. She looked forward to seeing Mary again. Lady

Cavendish intended to ask the Hollises to dine but there had not yet been an opportunity, nor for Diana to visit Mary.

When that day came, Lady Cavendish took it upon herself to pay her visit to the Duke of Eastleigh. She sent her card ahead, and as expected, he received her instantly.

She wasted no time in pleasantries but came straight to the point. "What folly is this I hear of you inviting the St Clairs to Eastleigh? And do not try to tell me you have developed any serious interest in sheep, rare breeds or otherwise. It will be obvious to anyone where your true interest lies."

The Duke, unfazed by Lady Cavendish's directness, misread her objection. "I know that they are not titled, but it is an old and noble family nonetheless."

Lady Cavendish made a disgusted noise that sounded not unlike "Pshaw!" Declining a glass offered to her by a servant, she attacked Eastleigh again. "It is not on your account that I have any reservations. I know that you are inclined towards marriage, but that girl is not for you. For starters, she is but half your age."

The Duke was shocked by this. After the confusion of having believed her to be a married woman, when he has supposed her to be at least twenty-two or three, he had given no thought to what her actual age might be. "How old is she?"

"She is but seventeen. Barely out of the schoolroom."

The Duke blanched. "Her manner is very much older."

"It may be, but that is a result of her upbringing. The St Clairs suffered considerable hardship for many years, and I have learnt that Miss St Clair assisted her mother in affairs of business. She was not thus sheltered from certain matters which a girl in her position is usually sheltered from. On the other hand, she has very little experience of society, for circumstances forced the family into seclusion."

Picturing Diana struggling in poverty merely made the Duke want to shower her with jewels. "Seventeen is not unmarriageable. And engagements may be of long duration," he said.

"It is not unmarriageable for a smart young man in his twenties, such as I have in mind for her. At your age, people would call you a second Ponsonby."

The Duke of Eastleigh took exception to this, though he knew Honoria Cavendish deliberately exaggerated. "Ponsonby is twenty years older than me."

"And you are twenty years older than Diana St Clair. There is the rub, sir, and I do not see how you can get past it."

But obstacles only make a lover more obstinate. "I have already written to Mrs St Clair to invite her to Eastleigh. I have no intention of withdrawing the invitation."

"Then more fool you. The place is an utter mausoleum. I can't imagine a young girl finding much to enjoy amid its relics, of which I number you among. I will take that drink," Lady Cavendish said, signalling to the servant. "My nerves are quite shaken."

The Duke failed to mask a smile. "Your nerves are never shaken, my lady."

"Were your mother alive, she would box your ears to put some sense into you."

"My mother was sixteen years younger than my father."

Honoria Cavendish had no comeback to this, for it was true, and the late Lord and Lady Beresford had enjoyed a very happy marriage. She still did not wish Diana to be buried under the weight of a duchy. She was daily impressed with the girl's insight and intelligence, and fancied modelling her into a younger version of herself. Honoria Cavendish had been a member of the Blue Stockings Society in her younger years. She considered that the world was all the more ready for driven, educated women than it had been in her day.

Diana had so much to tell Mary Hollis that she barely knew

where to begin. "So very many things have happened since I parted from you in Brighton. But first tell me how you have been. Is William well?"

"Nothing has changed for us," Mary replied, laughing. "It has not been so very long after all. But tell me your news, for I see that you can barely contain it. All is well with Lady Cavendish?"

"Very well. She is all kindness, and Lord Cavendish too. Yet only think! The Duke of Eastleigh came to the house and made me an apology. He was very contrite."

Mary considered this was only as it should have been. "After the inexcusable rudeness that you described from him, one would expect no less, duke or not." She had felt a personal indignation over the encounter, since it was her identity that the Duke had thought to malign.

"He was truly very sorry, and I felt quite pained on his behalf," Diana said.

"You show more forgiveness than most people would be capable of," Mary observed.

"But that is not all. He invited me to his house. Though he may not have meant it, for I have heard nothing since."

This led to a torrent of questions from Mary.

"He invited you to his house in London? Or to his country estate?" Diana confirmed that it was the latter. "What can he have meant by doing so? What is Lady Cavendish's view? She is aware, I suppose?"

Diana said that she was. "I do not know that she thought very much about it all. You see, it pertains to farming matters."

"Farming matters?!"

"To matters of sheep," Diana explained. "The Duke has heard about the rare breed that was bequeathed to my mother. And it appears that he also keeps rare breeds and thought we might be interested in their husbandry."

Mary was incredulous, even questioning whether her friend

might be delusional.

Matthew Hollis merely roared with laughter when his wife related the story to him later that evening, after Diana had returned to Mayfair.

"What is amusing about it?" Mary asked, as they dined on cold veal and ham pie. "Do you not find it curious that the Duke should take an interest in the St Clairs' sheep?"

"An interest in their sheep? I doubt the man gives two fiddles for their sheep. He has fallen for her, Mary dear, and the sheep were the best he could manage. I ought to take my hat off to him, were I wearing one. It is a highly original contrivance."

His wife was not convinced. "I hardly see how he can have developed an attachment to her. They had never spoken before the Cavendishes' ball. And she said he had always seemed very uncivil."

Matthew Hollis pointed out that this was only further evidence of his partiality. "A man who is indifferent to a woman does not invite her to his ancestral home for instruction in sheep-shearing."

Even Mrs St Clair was able to read between the lines to some degree, when the invitation to Eastleigh finally arrived. It had been delayed by some days due to a servant forgetting to forward it on from Orchard House to Bath.

"What can this mean, Jocasta? A duke whom I have never met invites us to his home to view his sheep. In Oxfordshire. Has he confused me with a livestock farmer? Does he wish to purchase Lord Harrogate's flock, perhaps?"

Maria and Henrietta were at this moment supervising the packing of their gowns, for they were to stay with their friends Miss Beasley and Mrs Petersham in Wells for a few days.

Jocasta Harcourt studied the invitation that her friend handed to her. "The Duke of Eastleigh, no less! I cannot say what this is about, but I have my doubts that his true purpose has anything to do with livestock."

Mrs St Clair recalled the name now. "Diana wrote to me of him once. As I recall she described him as very formidable and said that she was glad she need not marry him."

"He would be a superlative catch for any woman," Mrs Harcourt told her. "For he is handsome and exceedingly wealthy."

"I am sure I cannot regard this correspondence in the light of this being a catch for Diana, or for any of my girls. Yet it is Diana he invites. I can only suppose that this must be due to some influence of Lady Cavendish." Mrs St Clair had lately been troubled as to what the extent of this influence might be. The newspapers had recently linked Lady Cavendish to more than one controversial cause. Mrs St Clair was not sure that Diana should be exposed to it all.

"It comes at a convenient time," Jocasta Harcourt noted. "For though I shall miss your society here, at least your elder two have other plans with which to occupy themselves. Bath shall seem quite deserted without you all."

Mrs St Clair studied the invitation once more. "You think, then, that I should accept?"

"I would be all the more disappointed if you did not. But be cautious. Diana is young, but she attracted as much admiration as Henrietta when both were here, though neither of them knew it. I judged it wisest to say nothing."

Henrietta could not prevent a note of indignation on hearing that her young sister was invited to the home of a duke. "How all these titled introductions arose from a vicar's daughter, I am sure that I cannot say."

Maria agreed. "First Lady Cavendish and now the Duke of Eastleigh. It seems absurd that Mary Elford should have advanced to such circles."

Their mother recognised envy in her elder daughters but

held her tongue. "These strange coincidences do occur. And it may well be that his interest extends no further than our sheep."

Henrietta threw up her arms, having just realised there was a gown she had forgotten to have the maid pack with the rest. "I declare I am heartily sick of the sheep! The sooner they are all turned into a mutton pie, the better!"

CHAPTER 15

Having invited the girl and her mother to his estate, the Duke of Eastleigh was now troubled as to how the visit might go. He rarely entertained at Eastleigh, save for friends such as Montague Chalmers. The words of Lady Cavendish had stung. He was determined to show that Eastleigh was not a mausoleum and provide some lively amusements there.

It was to Monty he turned for advice.

"I have guests coming to Eastleigh in a fortnight. A Mrs St Clair and her daughter. I wondered if I should make up a party. Music, and dancing, perhaps."

Monty, who was excellent with names, remembered the three sisters that he had briefly met some weeks ago. They had been memorable, all three in bright gowns and very pretty if he recalled correctly. He wondered if these people were related. He wondered even more at his friend's motive in inviting them.

"It sounds an excellent plan. Your sister might act as hostess," he suggested, referring to Lady Julia, the daughter of the former duke's second wife.

The Duke, who had always viewed his half-sister as flighty, largely due to the preponderance of that quality in his late stepmother, agreed. "She is currently staying with an aunt of hers, but I shall have her return to Eastleigh."

Monty hoped this summons might be put to Lady Julia in a less autocratic tone. He was fond of the girl in an avuncular fashion and considered Eastleigh too high-handed with her. The Duke had already refused several requests for her hand in marriage. The late Dowager Duchess had been wealthy in her own right and her fortune had passed to her daughter on her death. Julia was thus a target for those with a pecuniary motive.

The Duke of Eastleigh had not resented his father marrying again, for his own mother had died when he was a small child. But he had not greatly approved of the late Duke's choice of bride. Letitia Lavenbrook, as she had been before her marriage, cared for little except partying and pleasure. There had barely been a moment's peace at Eastleigh during her time there.

When the former Duke had died, his widow had chosen to reside in London and continue her frivolity, rather than "entomb herself in the dower house", as she put it. This arrangement suited both her and her stepson very well, though the Duke would never have made her unwelcome at Eastleigh and had maintained the dower house for her use.

But she was never to return to it. Her Grace the Dowager Duchess of Eastleigh died suddenly of a fever, not two years after her husband. Despite his personal view of his stepmother, the current Duke had felt genuine sorrow on behalf of his sister. He had been made Julia's legal guardian and took this duty seriously. But his household was lonely for a young woman, and as Julia had grown up and made her debut, she generally preferred to reside with other friends and relatives.

"Lady Julia might also be prevailed upon to bring some friends with her. You will need a good number of young people if there is to be dancing," Monty observed. "Most importantly, the ladies should not too greatly outnumber the men, so they need not be forced to sit out."

The Duke had an unnerving feeling that left to Monty and Julia, the thing might spiral into a huge rout. Which was not his intention. Were he to be overwhelmed with guests, there would be a loss of intimacy with those with whom he particularly wished to be intimate.

'You'll never guess whom I encountered the other night at White's," Monty said as they dined on roast venison with an excellent claret.

The Duke could not guess, so waited for his friend to continue.

"Old Eames. And you know whom he's acting for? Ponsonby, in the Crim Con trial. Courtroom ought to be crowded to excess. The lady won't be there, of course, nor the Captivating Comte, as they've dubbed him. But there's a score of witnesses expected."

It was not a subject which the Duke wished to discuss, but he did not want to convey this to Montague. For it might arouse questions. Monty had an ear for gossip and the Duke usually indulged him.

"Naturally there's little sympathy for Ponsonby," Monty continued. "But there's no fool like an old fool, as they say. Her parents are to blame as much, in my view. For there's a word for that arrangement, and it ain't a pretty one. Marriage bonds and the church's sanction regardless."

It got worse. Monty became fired up about his theme, assuming his friend to be in agreement with it.

"All very well for a man to delay matrimony. But it's not the thing to go after such a young chit. Not at his age."

The Duke felt defensive enough to protest. "There are many couples who are far apart in age who seem perfectly content with their situation. My own mother was fourteen years my father's junior. And Hatton was a decade younger than his wife."

"I fear they are the exceptions," Monty said. "Besides, there were over three decades between the Ponsonbys. You must own the absurdity of that."

"She could have refused him," the Duke pointed out, then regretted doing so, for it only prolonged the painful topic.

"Easier said than done. They say her father was threatened with Marshalsea," Monty revealed, referring to a notorious debtor's prison.

The Duke was troubled enough to start regretting his plans. There was now certainly no way he could confide in Monty about his intentions. How his purpose in inviting the St Clair girl down was to establish a better acquaintance with a view to offering for her.

She is but seventeen. Honoria Cavendish was right. He was no better than Ponsonby.

Well, the invitation was sent now. But it was not too late to avoid complete humiliation. He would confine himself to playing the hospitable host, nothing more. The role of suitor must be left to a younger man.

Diana, still with Lady Cavendish, had supposed nothing more would come of the Duke's invitation. She was surprised when a letter came from her mother confirming the arrangements. Mrs St Clair had written to both Lady Cavendish and Diana, but her letter to her daughter revealed more of her own thoughts.

"You have not mentioned the Duke of Eastleigh in your recent letters, so I was unaware of any acquaintance. I have accepted on your behalf, but if you are unhappy with the idea and prefer to remain in London, we may still make some excuse. Jocasta Harcourt suggests that we meet at a particular coaching inn in Oxford - the Three Bells - and from there travel together to his estate, which is some miles to the south. I shall arrange a carriage so you only need hire a post chaise as far as Oxford."

Lady Cavendish had concealed from Diana her disapproval of the Duke's behaviour. She was aware that Diana had no idea of his intentions but suspected that Mrs St Clair would be better able to detect them. She assumed Mrs St Clair to be a refined and sensible woman, given her daughter's qualities.

"What is Eastleigh like?" Diana asked, having finished reading the latest political reports to Lady Cavendish. "I mean the estate, not the Duke."

"Very large and very old, and some might say very grand,"

Lady Cavendish told her. "The late dowager duchess frequently entertained, but even with a hundred chandeliers it always felt dark and austere to me. Historically, I suppose, it is very interesting," she conceded.

Dark and austere. It was how Diana viewed the Duke, and she could not help a faint shiver.

She had found herself quite desperate to see him again, though she knew not why. He had been inexcusably rude to her, he had endlessly glared at her, yet despite it all she wanted his approval.

To this end she had determined not to appear foolish or ignorant. When Lady Cavendish took her to Hatchard's Bookshop, Diana managed to find a pamphlet on the selective breeding of sheep, which she purchased and studied diligently.

Lord Cavendish had been amused by Diana's choice of reading material. He had been pleased to have her as a guest in his home, not just because she usefully occupied his wife. But the girl was also exceptionally pretty with a very attractive voice. She was certainly a decorative addition to his dinner table, at any rate.

He produced some old editions of the Annals of Agriculture for her. "These were in my library. I fear they are rather outdated. You may take them for as long you like, for I have no need of them."

By the time the date of her journey to Oxford arrived, Diana felt herself quite a scholar. She knew her dewlap from her top knot and her teg from her gimmer.

Arriving at the appointed inn in Oxford, Diana was overjoyed to be reunited with her mother for she had missed her very much. Letters were not the same. Mrs St Clair's health had continued to improve in the time they had spent apart. She and Jenny, who accompanied her, both looked well despite the long journey from Bath.

Diana was keen for news of her sisters who were not diligent correspondents. "They are staying with friends in Wells, so this invitation to Eastleigh has all been very convenient," her mother told her.

"Which friends were those?"

"A Miss Beasley and a Mrs Petersham. Did you know them during your time in Bath?"

Diana said that she did, and then said nothing more. For she could not think of anything very favourable to say about those women.

Mrs St Clair managed to raise a subject that had been troubling her. "My dear, you will forgive me if I intrude, but is there some sort of understanding between you and His Grace?"

From the way her daughter's mouth dropped open, Mrs St Clair gathered there was not.

"I do not think he even likes me, mamma. I have not written of everything to you, but there was a misunderstanding at Lady Cavendish's ball, where he mistook me for someone else. I believe he invites us to make amends," Diana said.

"A misunderstanding?" Mrs St Clair looked concerned.

Diana did not want to revisit the encounter but knew her mother might be even more worried by imagining what had taken place. "Only that I danced with someone, and the Duke mistook me for a married woman, and spoke somewhat harshly to me. But as soon as he discovered his error, he apologised."

This was not a very accurate representation of the facts, and it left Mrs St Clair even more puzzled. "Harsh words? Was there something to reprimand in your conduct?"

"I do not think so. For if there had been, Lady Cavendish would surely not have invited me back into her home. And Mary Hollis did not think I behaved in any way untoward. I suppose it is that married women do not dance as much as unmarried women."

"Even so, my dear, it is not a matter for public censure if they do. But you say he has apologised, so we will speak no further of it. He is to be our host, after all."

CHAPTER 16

Eastleigh did indeed seem an austere and even ominous edifice when their carriage drove up at dusk.

It loomed large and dark, with flickers of light at some of the windows.

"I am told the grounds are very elegant," Mrs St Clair said, attempting to conceal her own apprehension.

They were admitted by a liveried footman, and greeted by the Duke himself, who had stepped into the hall on hearing their vehicle arrive.

His greeting and the polite conventions of the occasion passed in a blur for Diana, who let her mother manage most of the exchange. Diana found herself conscious of how dishevelled she must look from the journey. It had never bothered her before, since one cannot expect to emerge uncrumpled from a long carriage ride.

But the Duke was always so impeccably dressed that Diana felt unease in his presence.

"I am very glad you could come," he said to her, and there was genuine warmth in his voice.

He introduced them to his half-sister, and Diana was instantly taken with Lady Julia. Tall, with auburn hair, she had a look in her eye that reminded her of Susannah Lewis. Outwardly she deferred to her brother at each point, but Diana could tell that she was not as meek as she was pretending.

She was less taken with a Miss Isabella Wilde, introduced to her as a friend of Lady Julia. Miss Wilde had a haughtiness to her that reminded Diana of her sister Maria. She was several years older than Lady Julia - Diana put her age at about eight-and-twenty, whereas the Duke's sister did not appear to be much older than she herself was, perhaps a year or two, but no more. There were two other women, Miss Laura Selcome and Miss Lydia Selcome. They were the type who giggled when nervous, Diana observed.

There were not any men present except for the Duke, but they learnt that this was because the male guests were currently visiting the Duke's stables. He had recently acquired a well-known racehorse for breeding stock and the men had been eager to see it.

"I dare say they will be back soon, for it grows dark. I do not know why they could not have waited until tomorrow, but you know how gentleman can be with horses," Lady Julia said. "Mrs Perkins will show you to your rooms. I am sure you must be fatigued from your long journey, so if you would prefer to dine privately, just let her know. Otherwise I will have someone sent to take you to the dining room, for this house is a veritable labyrinth."

Diana and Mrs St Clair had been given adjoining rooms. The furniture was very old, dark and heavy, but of a fine quality. Everything had been well cared for, but not modernised.

"It is not quite the castle of Udolpho, but I am very glad that there are plenty of people about. For I should not like to be here on a lonely winter's night," Diana said. "How did you find the Duke of Eastleigh?"

"On such a brief acquaintance I cannot fairly give much opinion, save for he displays excellent manners and appears to be a courteous host. He is certainly a very fine looking man," Mrs St Clair said.

"I thought his sister very charming."

"Indeed. She does not greatly resemble him in appearance, though she is also very fine looking. She is his half-sister, I believe?"

Diana was not sure. She shared her mother's view of Lady

Julia's looks, considering her to be quite beautiful. Miss Wilde was also handsome, and the Selcome sisters were pretty.

It was all quite overwhelming but Diana was excited rather than daunted. Conscious of her mother's delicate health she suggested that they take a tray in their rooms. But Mrs St Clair assured her daughter that she felt quite robust and would be happy to dine in company.

What fine company it was! The male members of the party also numbered six. Apart from the Duke of Eastleigh there were his friend Mr Montague Chalmers, whom Diana vaguely remembered from Bath, and a Mr Ravenscroft, a thin, dark man with a cynical wit. The Duke had also invited his cousin, the Honourable Frederick Fulham, who had brought two friends with him. These were a Mr Henry Tanqueray, cut very much from the same cloth as the Honourable Frederick, and - to Diana's surprise and delight - Charles Lewis.

"Cha... Mr Lewis, I did not expect to see you here," she greeted him.

"Nor I you," Charles said, the expression on his own face no less pleased.

"You two are already acquainted?" Frederick said. "That's all to the good, then. Saves time on all these blighted introductions. Lewis here backed me where you wouldn't, cousin," he said to the Duke. "Successfully too, for I beat Albemarle by two lengths. That new nag of yours looks to have some spirit in him. I wonder how he'd go in a thing like that new high-flyer we saw at Felton's?" This remark was aimed at Mr Tanqueray, who shared his friend's passion for racing.

"I have no idea, nor do I intend to find out," the Duke told him. "Your latest phaeton is death trap enough." He had observed the delight with which Diana greeted the young Lewis fellow, and felt himself gripped by some emotion that was nearly painful.

Diana was also happy to be seated by Charles Lewis at dinner. "How is Susannah?" she asked.

"She is very well, though we have all missed you in Bath," Charles said. "She was thinking to go up to town and hoped to call on you. But tell me, what brought you here? Is Eastleigh not the same Duke whom you claimed frowned upon you?"

"It is a very long story, and not one I can easily relate here," Diana said, hoping that they were not in earshot of the Duke. He appeared to be engaged in conversation with her mother at that moment, who was seated on one side of him, with Isabella Wilde on the other. "Suffice it to say that you were near the mark when you suggested a confusion of identity, though I am still not sure how that arose in Bath. Now it is all resolved, I believe he has asked me here as some sort of gesture."

Charles, more worldly than Diana and as a man far more aware of her attractions, privately doubted this. But he had not noticed Eastleigh paying her any special attentions. "I confess that you had piqued my curiosity about him, after what you told Susannah and me in Bath. It was partly due to that that I accepted Fulham's invitation. I wondered what sort of a man his cousin might be."

"I believe he is a very noble and decent man," Diana said, casting a gaze at the elegant head in question. The Duke briefly caught her eye, and she felt as though something unspoken passed between them.

"Let us hope that he is decent enough to put on some entertainment equal to the magnificence of his dinner. For it seems months since we danced."

Diana agreed that the food was excellent, practically a banquet she thought, though she had not ever attended such a meal. There were many courses, ranging from the familiar to the exotic, and bowls overflowing with fresh fruit from the forcing house.

Amid the many candles, and the warmer decor of the dining

room, Eastleigh and its master seemed less formidable.

There was no dancing that evening, for the Duke did not wish to overtax those guests who had travelled some long distances to Eastleigh, Diana and Mrs St Clair among them. When the ladies retired, Diana found herself in a charming salon decorated in pale blue, white and gold.

Admiring it, she discovered it to be the work of the late Dowager Duchess, with her praise pleasing Lady Julia. "My brother did not always greatly approve of my mother - his stepmother - but it cannot be doubted that she did a great deal to improve Eastleigh. And the late duke's first wife as well. I can only imagine how dismaying this place must have been to a young bride. You need not wonder why I stay away."

"It is very impressive though, and must be very historic," Diana said.

Lady Julia shuddered. "I vastly prefer the comforts of town. When I was a child I was quite convinced it was haunted. Which indeed it may well be. Though I am sure any phantom would be more terrified of my brother in one of his fiercer moods, than the reverse."

This was said in jest. But it was some effort for Diana, who had been at the receiving end of such a mood, to smile back.

She found the Selcome sisters less shy than her first assumption, though it may have been that they were more relaxed in the company of women. Miss Wilde was more reserved. And though Diana had resolved not to think the worst of anyone, she could not help but feel that that lady regarded her with some disdain.

But Lady Julia's charm and warmth more than made up for the absence of it in her friend. Diana also learnt that Lady Julia's companion, a Miss Etteridge, was among the household, but had retired early due to a headache.

"Poor Ettie. I suspect that she would not have stayed down, headache or not. For we would then have been thirteen to dine, and she is very superstitious," Lady Julia told Diana. Her green eyes glinted. "If you are ever forced to have a companion, be sure to engage some very elderly woman. For their eyesight is less acute - at least if you hide their spectacles - and they are in the habit of napping. It affords much better opportunity for private conversation with friends, when one's companion is snoring in her chair."

With confidences such as this, the two young women were soon firm friends.

CHAPTER 17

Diana awoke early the next morning. She had feared she might lie awake for hours, hearing the groans of a ghost flailing through the passages. But tired from the journey and having met so many people, she fell asleep very quickly. Her one regret of the evening was that the Duke had not spoken very much to her.

She was not sure if it was appropriate to stay in her room until some sort of summons and she did not want to wake her mother. But the morning was so fine and the view of the surrounding countryside so appealing that she longed for more fresh air than the casement window, with its stiff hinges, permitted.

They had all been in the habit of rising early at Didmarton, for even candles had been an expense. Making the most of the free light of day was one way to economise.

Hoping that she did not commit any transgression, Diana dressed and made her way down the wide staircase. There was a footman already in attendance in the hall, but he made no objection to her presence, instead offering to guide her to the morning room.

This was a salon painted in the lightest rose and cream, with large vases of flowers and the sun streaming in through the easterly aspect. Diana was relieved and pleased to find Lady Julia already there.

"Miss St Clair! Good morning. How fortunate that I am not the only one to have risen early. Would you like some refreshments, or to take a turn about the grounds? For it is such a fine morning, and to remain inside makes me feel positively entombed!" Lady Julia declared.

Diana was glad to go for a walk. Lady Julia led her along a sunny path, showing her the various gardens and commenting on changes to them over the past years. Gradually her conversation became more intimate, with her questioning Diana as to how she and her mother had made the Duke's acquaintance.

"It was at Lady Cavendish's house in Sussex," Diana told her.

"Lady Cavendish? She is quite formidable, is she not? I have only met her on two or three occasions, and I am sure that I positively quailed in her presence."

Diana even on her brief acquaintance with Lady Julia, could not imagine her quailing at anything.

"How on earth did my brother manage to persuade you to come to Eastleigh?" Lady Julia continued.

Diana recognised this for an attempt to discover why the Duke had invited them, not why they had accepted. "My family owns a rare breed of sheep, Cotswold Longhorns, an interest which His Grace apparently shares."

Lady Julia stopped and stared at Diana. "Sheep?"

"Yes. He mentioned that he has several rare breeds here and thought we might be interested to learn more of their husbandry."

Lady Julia was now looking at Diana as though Diana herself had sprouted a pair of long horns. "I cannot recall my brother ever mentioning sheep in his life. He is not even particularly fond of mutton."

Diana was bewildered. "Perhaps it may be a more recent interest? There are sheep at Eastleigh, are there not?"

"I suppose so, in a field somewhere perhaps. I can't say I have ever thought about it." Lady Julia was silent for a few moments and Diana worried that the topic of sheep had annoyed her. But then Lady Julia addressed her again. "You will forgive me for asking, Miss St Clair, but how old are you?

I am sure we cannot be too far apart in age, so I hope the question does not offend you."

"Not at all. I turned seventeen last July," Diana told her.

"I confess I am surprised, for you have a very composed manner and I had thought you must be older than me. I will be twenty in August, which is still tiresomely far from my majority. Isabella will be relieved, at any rate."

"Miss Wilde?" Diana did not understand the connection.

"She was convinced my brother must have intentions towards you and was very irritated about it. For she has long held hopes of that herself. If I may be very frank with you, she is not a very close friend of mine, nor do I care greatly for her company. But Monty - Mr Chalmers, he has been Monty to me since I was a child - once let slip that my brother considered her a suitable candidate for his duchess. So I brought her down here, for it is high time that he married. Especially after negotiations with the Amberforths appear to have come to nothing. For once he finally takes a wife, he will have enough to occupy himself without interfering endlessly in my affairs."

Diana's head was spinning at these revelations. They might at least account for Isabella Wilde's coolness towards her. "I hope I have said nothing to give that impression to Miss Wilde."

"Oh, you did not at all. But she has waited for long that I suppose she is anxious of any rival. For my part, I would rather have you as a sister-in-law than her, so the prospect did not trouble me. But being only seventeen, my brother could not possibly have any intentions towards you," Lady Julia explained.

"He does not consider seventeen a marriageable age?" Diana asked.

"Not for someone of his years. I shouldn't think anyone does after the Ponsonby scandal. For my part I commend her. I should do exactly the same if I were forced into marrying some lecherous old goat."

They turned a corner, with Lady Julia remarking a spot on which her mother had wanted to plant a rose garden. "A sort of pergola affair. Only the gardener said the aspect was all wrong, something to do with the wind." Then she abruptly changed the subject. "Mr Lewis is very handsome, is he not?"

"Indeed," Diana replied.

"It is a pity he is not titled. Not that such things mean anything to me, but they do to my brother. He is not a snob, you understand, only he is always worried about aspirants."

Diana felt aggrieved on Charles's behalf. "Mr Lewis is not an aspirant."

"Oh, I am quite sure he is not. It is just my brother's perpetual suspicion. I became so annoyed by it that last year I feigned an attachment to someone I knew he would find totally unsuitable. Goodness only knows what he threatened the poor fellow with, for I never heard from him again. It happens that I have no intention of marrying just yet, though my brother does not know it. But it served him right to go to the trouble he did, for my private affairs should be none of his business," Lady Julia said.

Diana recalled her conversation with Charles and Susannah where all three had felt sympathy for the Duke's sister. Such sympathy she now realised had been misplaced. The Duke of Eastleigh might be overbearing, but his sister was certainly not to be overborne.

Montague Chalmers could not imagine how he had failed to remark on the quite dazzling beauty of Miss St Clair on his earlier encounter with her in Bath. It was true, he had been distracted by the task of disentangling Frederick, but the girl was an absolute diamond of the first water.

Monty was quite certain that the Duke was not unaware of the girl's allure either. There had to be some reason for his sudden and mysterious invitation of these people, for the Duke rarely entertained at his country house. Now Monty sensed he had discovered it. He had probed Julia earlier, when he had sat beside her at breakfast. She had revealed some strange tale concerning sheep. Monty shared her incredulity. He could not for the life of him imagine Eastleigh being remotely interested in Mrs St Clair's flock when she had a daughter like Diana.

It might also go some way to explaining Eastleigh's odd defensiveness over the topic of the Ponsonby marriage. For the St Clair girl was several years younger than the other females he had been considering. Miss Wilde had looked quite put out, Monty thought. Though he was uncertain why the Duke should invite her if he had designs on the younger girl.

In his view, Isabella Wilde would be no better a choice than Lady Jane had been. Monty did not greatly care for Miss Wilde, though he accepted she was handsome and came from impeccable lineage. It was a troublesome thing, matrimony. Once you made your choice you were stuck with it, bar a convenient bereavement or an Act of Parliament. No, he himself would not be rushing into such a state of affairs any time soon.

The Misses Selcome turned out to be not as timid as Diana's first impression of them. They did have a propensity to titter when flustered, and it took little to fluster them. But they both played and sang very well. Laura Selcome even revealed that she was uninterested in matrimony but hoped to open a girls' school.

"A progressive academy for young ladies. Where they might not only learn the graces of art, literature and music, but also become accomplished in more practical areas of knowledge. For a woman may not always rely on a man's wisdom and judgment when it comes to her own private affairs," she said.

Her sister agreed. "We know of widows who have been

quite defrauded by ill-intentioned advice."

Diana shared her own experience in helping manage her family's finances, and the sisters nodded in agreement.

"Precisely so. We may be the weaker sex, but that does not mean we need be the weak-minded sex," Lydia Selcome pointed out.

Charles Lewis was also all encouragement. "I see no reason why a woman should not be knowledgeable and capable when it comes to her own financial affairs. When my grandfather built his business in the early days, my grandmother kept his books. She had a far greater head for figures than he did," he told her. "I must attribute our family's fortune at least partly to her good sense."

All in all it was a very pleasant day, with people touring the grounds and discoursing with one another. Mrs St Clair and Miss Etteridge, Lady Julia's companion, were happy to sit in the shade of a willow while the younger people amused themselves.

The Honourable Frederick and Mr Tanqueray were mostly absorbed in discussion of racing and horses. Diana found Mr Ravenscroft to be very knowledgeable about music, something she herself was not, but found interesting as a subject.

Charles Lewis was particularly entertaining, and Diana could not help but observe that Lady Julia attached herself to him at every opportunity. Other than the Duke, he was by far the most attractive gentleman there.

"Do you ride, Miss St Clair?" Lady Julia asked, when they were shown the stables and the Duke's new horse.

Diana was sorry to say that she did not.

"It is nothing to be sorry for. I am not very fond of it myself. It is so much more pleasant to be driven in a carriage, do you not think? One may relax and talk with far greater ease. It allows for more intimate friendship." This last was said with a mischievous glance towards Charles Lewis.

"I am sure I should fear to go driving with you, Lady Julia, lest you prise all my secrets from me," he replied.

"What an unjust supposition! And how may I prove you wrong, if you refuse me admission to your carriage?" Lady Julia said.

"I do not say that I refuse, only that I find myself extremely wary at the prospect," Charles said.

Lady Julia's pointed flirtation naturally resulted in Charles Lewis offering to take her for a drive, as had clearly been her intention. This led to Frederick Fulham proposing a carriage race followed by a picnic, and offering a case of claret from his cousin's cellar to the winner. Since Frederick had the fastest phaeton and two new stallions, there was little doubt about the outcome of such a contest.

"I do not think we need make a race of it. But if the weather holds, we may arrange a picnic," the Duke offered.

A lively discussion of destinations ensued. There was a split between those who wanted to go to some nearby ruins, and others who preferred the top of an adjacent hill.

"It is gloomy in the forest and windy on the hill," Lady Julia observed. "We ought to go to Abbey Lake, for it is scenic there but offers the shelter of willows if the sun is harsh."

"What do you think, Miss St Clair?"

Diana was startled to find herself thus addressed by the Duke, for he had barely spoken a word to her all day. Most of his conversation had been with the other gentlemen and Miss Wilde. Diana supposed this was natural, if there were an understanding between them, and tried not to resent it. There was no reason why he should pay her any more attention than he did to the Misses Selcome.

"The lake sounds very lovely," Diana replied, for it did, and she thought it politic to side with Lady Julia.

"Then the lake it is," the Duke of Eastleigh confirmed. "I

will have arrangements made. If it rains, we will devise some other amusements."

The Duke had observed the relaxed conversation between his sister, Diana and Charles Lewis. Irrationally he felt excluded even though he had chosen to distance himself. He silently cursed Frederick for bringing the Lewis fellow, for he suspected that Charles Lewis had clear designs on Diana St Clair.

Accompanied by Monty, the Duke went to view an ancient oak that was due to be felled. The tree was rotten to a hollow inside. There was no real need to see it, for he had approved the felling, but it was an excuse to escape the rest of the party.

"It must have been a magnificent specimen in its day," Monty observed.

"I climbed it as a boy. There were still leaves on it then, it is but a skeleton now."

The two men walked around the oak, regarding its decayed form and paying silent homage to the great tree.

"Some five hundred years or more it has stood here. Older than the house and the duchy itself," the Duke observed.

As they walked back through the park, Monty decided to do some digging. He was still curious about Eastleigh's motive for hosting the gathering.

"Your guests appear to be amusing themselves well," he began. "It is some years since Eastleigh saw a jaunt like this. Not since your stepmother's day, I'll warrant."

"Letitia was fond of company," the Duke said.

"Your sister brought along some pretty fillies. And the Wilde girl among them. Do I take it that she has moved up the list?"

The Duke felt mildly irritated. If the past two days had taught him anything, it was that he was hugely relieved not to have become entangled with Isabella Wilde. He had found her false and supercilious.

"I have no intentions towards her," he said.

Monty probed further. "The St Clair girl is uncommonly lovely. No wonder she was such a hit in Bath." Did he imagine it, or did Eastleigh stiffen at the mention of her name? He continued: "I was not aware you were acquainted with her there."

"I was not. The introduction came via Honoria Cavendish," the Duke informed his friend. He gave no further explanation, which only encouraged Monty to supply his own. Eastleigh had always been open when they had discussed marriage prospects. His current reserve was intriguing.

Monty said no more on the subject, not wishing to rattle his friend further. Instead he shared an amusing anecdote he had heard regarding a mutual acquaintance, and the mood between them was once again companionable by the time they returned to the house.

CHAPTER 18

That night there was dancing after dinner. They were too few for the main ballroom, but another salon, with some rearrangement of furniture, proved the ideal size.

For Monty, the dancing would put his theory to the test that Eastleigh had an interest in Diana St Clair. The Duke rarely if ever danced, so if he did that evening, it would be a clear sign that something was up.

Diana chose to wear her white silk dress again. The time spent outdoors had freshened her complexion and she looked as well as she had ever done. That evening she had been seated between Mr Ravenscroft and Mr Tanqueray and had done her best to be polite to Miss Wilde, who still appeared to disdain her.

The Duke had hired musicians, whose performance was enriched by both the Selcome sisters and Mr Ravenscroft taking turns at piano accompaniment.

Diana was flattered that Charles Lewis asked her for the first dance, which was a vigorous Scots Reel. She did not know if their host would dance for he had not done so at the Cavendish ball. And she had never seen him dancing in Bath. But if he should dance, Diana secretly prayed that he might ask her at least once.

This happy moment came during the waltz, which Diana had been forced to sit out. Mr Ravenscroft was at the piano; Charles Lewis danced with Lady Julia, Montague Chalmers with Isabella, and Frederick and Mr Tanqueray with the Selcomes.

"You are without a partner, Miss St Clair? I hope you may allow me to remedy that."

Without waiting for her response the Duke offered her his arm and led her among the other dancing couples. Diana was greatly surprised, for the Duke had not yet danced with anyone.

Feeling his arms about her, even though it were only done as the convention of the dance, made her feel dizzy. This close she could smell the aroma of his skin: a clean, masculine aroma with a trace of frankincense and forest leaves.

She dared not look up at him lest he see her blushes. It was all she could do to remember the steps.

The Duke moved with a powerful grace. He guided her, preventing her from stumbling once or twice. Diana, normally a graceful dancer, felt unforgivably clumsy. At one point she began to apologise but he smiled and, she fancied, grasped her even more tightly.

This close to him she found it hard to swallow. Even to breathe. As the music ended, the Duke looked down at her. "The heat of the room overcomes you, I fear. It is a warm night. Come, we will take a moment of fresh air."

Nervous but exhilarated to be thus singled out, Diana allowed the Duke to escort her to the small terrace that opened from the room. Surrounded by a balustrade, it overlooked the now-darkened gardens of Eastleigh and the parkland and woods beyond.

"You are enjoying yourself?" the Duke asked her.

"Very much so, your Grace. Eastleigh is quite magnificent."

"Some find it gloomy and overly large."

Diana thought for a moment before replying. "I think it is a house that may take some getting used to, but overall I think its size becomes it." She hoped he would not find this too critical.

But he laughed, a soft, low laugh, and she realised it was the first time she had ever heard him laugh. Something inside her seemed to dissolve at the sound.

"Why do you think I have brought you here, Miss St Clair?"

"For some air?"

"I mean to Eastleigh," the Duke said.

"You mentioned that you wished us to see your sheep," Diana said. Her throat felt constricted and it was difficult to form even these words. In the moonlight he was taller and darker than ever, the glow of candlelight from within the room casting a dim radiance over his features. She felt that she never wanted to leave this spot, but just to gaze at him. All his earlier angry glares at her were forgotten.

For now, as he looked down at her, there was such an expression of tenderness in his eyes that it obliterated all else.

His voice was low. "It was only part of the reason I wished you to come to Eastleigh."

They stood there, gazing at one another. Diana was not sure what was happening to her. She only knew that she desired to remain in his proximity. She could have stood there for a hundred years.

A strange heat seemed to flow through her body. She did not know what she wanted, but she wanted more. Closer.

The Duke reached out a hand and his fingers traced the side of her face. Her skin tingled from his touch even after the contact ended. It was as though he had marked a pattern there. Diana could not breathe.

He spoke again. "You are very young, my dear."

Amid the tenderness she saw a strange regret in his eyes, and feared that she had done something wrong, or failed to do or say something he wanted.

The Duke ached to take her in his arms. He could not have done so even if he had thought she would respond, for it would have compromised them both. For the terrace was overlooked from the room. And even if it were not, he hoped he were not so low as to seduce an innocent maiden.

She had trembled as he touched her. Blinded by love and his own passion, he mistook it for fear rather than desire. At once remorse overcame him, and he knew he must step back.

She was so grave and still. He recalled her laughing ease with the other gentlemen, and the strange new pain came back to him. Yet he gazed upon her a moment longer, regretting his own years and her lack of years, and wishing that men like Charles Lewis did not exist.

He was about to escort her back into the room when they were joined by two of his other guests: Isabella Wilde and Montague Chalmers.

"The night air is refreshing, is it not?" Miss Wilde said.

"It is a warmer evening than I had foreseen," the Duke said. "I fear this salon, with its western aspect, is ill-suited to dancing on such a night."

"For my part I find the dancing quite delightful," Miss Wilde told him, and he realised he would be forced to ask her to dance. Now he had danced with one woman, for courtesy's sake he must offer to dance with them all. All the more so as host.

Monty was regarding his friend with some private amusement. He could see that Eastleigh was irritated to have been interrupted. Monty's suspicions were more than confirmed. Not just by this, but by the way the Duke had danced with the St Clair girl and then led her outside for private conversation.

He was not the only one. Miss Wilde had practically dragged Monty to the terrace as well, conscious of a rival. She was all smiles and charm, but there was ice beneath it.

"Perhaps I may claim you for the next measure, Miss St Clair?" Monty asked, noticing Eastleigh's jaw clench in reaction.

The Duke then had to offer the same invitation to Miss Wilde, at which point all four re-entered the room. The musicians struck up a gavotte, and everyone took their places. The Duke tried to concentrate on his partner and not let his eyes wander too frequently to Diana, but it was not easy.

Mrs St Clair had also noticed the Duke singling out her daughter. She was not overly surprised, for she had never been particularly convinced by the sheep. It had struck her from the first that he must have some other motive. Nonetheless she was troubled, for Diana had very little experience with men. Mrs St Clair had hoped that her youngest daughter would have at least a couple of seasons before making her choice.

She knew nothing of the Duke of Eastleigh personally. While he seemed to be an upright and well-meaning man, he might well have nothing more in mind than flirtation. After all he was a duke, and Diana had no title nor family connections. A girl could survive a broken heart. But Mrs St Clair did not want to see her daughter suffering unnecessary pain.

Charles Lewis, a straightforward young man and nearer Diana's age, would have been a far better choice. But he was being all but monopolised by Lady Julia, to whose attentions he showed little resistance.

"Your daughter dances very well," Miss Etteridge, seated nearby, remarked.

Mrs St Clair thanked her. "All the young people make a pretty spectacle, do they not? It is good of His Grace to provide such entertainment. The musicians are very fine."

"Indeed they are. How well the Misses Selcome sing and play as well! They are most accomplished."

Agreeing, Mrs St Clair wondered if she should have words with Diana about the Duke, but ultimately decided not to. Her daughter had not expressed any romantic interest in the Duke, and it might be nothing more than a passing fancy on his part.

Charles Lewis had not noticed the Duke and Diana. While he still had a preference for Diana above all other young women, he had been distracted by the attentions of Lady Julia.

Charles was experienced enough to guess that her flirtation might at least in part be to goad her brother. But it was hard not to be flattered. Cynical though he was, her persistence resulted in mutual admiration.

He reasoned that Diana had not returned any clear signs of affection beyond a warm friendship. Whereas Lady Julia was relentless in her teasing and flirting. Charles made sure to dance with all the women there, though the Misses Selcome were not his sort at all. He had not greatly taken to Isabella Wilde either, finding her manner condescending.

The evening eventually drew to a close, as people retired. Frederick, Charles, Mr Tanqueray and Montague Chalmers made up a foursome to play cards but everyone else retired to their chambers.

Alone in her room, Diana longed for a friend such as Susannah Lewis or Mary Hollis, in whom she might have confided. For her emotions were all over the place. She had felt elation and fear, joy and disappointment. She thought she had never felt such happiness as when she danced with the Duke, nor such dejection as when he danced with Miss Wilde.

But she reminded herself of her place. She must not interpret his behaviour as anything more than the courtesy of a host. From Lady Julia she knew that the Duke's intentions were towards Isabella Wilde, and they might well already have a private understanding.

She gazed at the moon through the casement window, thinking that it had never looked so lovely nor so lonely.

CHAPTER 19

The Duke refused to let the Honourable Frederick transport any of the women in his "break-neck of a vehicle" to the picnic site. The weather had turned out fine, which meant arranging carriages and horses to transport everyone. As a result Frederick drove with Mr Tanqueray, vowing that they would "go the long way around and still arrive an hour before the others".

It was a reduced party that headed to Abbey Lake. Mr Ravenscroft and the Misses Selcome preferred to remain behind, having plans to play music as a trio. Mrs St Clair and Miss Etteridge had found some common interests and were also happy to stay behind. A long carriage ride through open country on a hot day held little appeal to either.

This meant that the picnickers numbered five gentlemen and three ladies. Lady Julia insisted on being driven by Charles Lewis, claiming he had promised this the previous day.

That left Diana, Isabella Wilde, the Duke and Monty to take the coach. Miss Wilde had initially rejected this plan, claiming that a gig would be more pleasant on such a fine day. But the Duke, wary of ending up driving the lady himself which he suspected was her aim, made a compelling case for the larger vehicle.

"The coach will offer far more comfort along the country roads, which are dusty and frequently uneven," the Duke said. He then manoeuvred the seating so that he was placed next to Diana.

It took an hour and a half to reach the lake. Conversation was largely the effort of Montague Chalmers, for the other three were absorbed in their own thoughts.

As she sat next to the Duke, Diana felt the same constriction in her throat that she had done the previous night. His thigh was so near to her own that she could feel the warmth of it. Whenever the carriage ran over a bump in the road, she was jostled against him. He had not spoken to her personally that morning and she had fancied he was avoiding her.

Miss Wilde's thoughts may easily be guessed. She was seething with annoyance that Julia had managed to secure herself intimacy with Charles Lewis, while she herself had failed to obtain a private ride with the Duke. Instead that detestable St Clair girl was once again usurping her place. She would have to nip that situation in the bud. It would not be difficult, for the girl was very green and doubtless had very little experience in romantic affairs.

The Duke was himself frustrated that Isabella Wilde's attempts to drive alone with him had thwarted his own intentions to do so with Diana. For he could hardly insist on the comfort of a carriage and then take Diana in the gig. Sitting next to her in the company of Monty and Miss Wilde was a very poor second to his original hopes. He was also wondering how he might get her alone at the lake. He suspected doing so would involve having to shake off the persistent Isabella. Julia be damned for bringing the woman here! Yet he could not display any discourtesy, for his father had been a great friend of Sir George Wilde.

Monty, who needed no psychic gifts to perceive his fellow passengers' thoughts, was greatly entertained. Knowing the area well, he deliberately made various observations as they travelled along, to which only Miss St Clair had the courtesy to offer much response.

"We now pass through Lower Revesby, where to the left you can glimpse the Norman church tower behind those trees," he said.

Diana leant forward so that she might look out of the far

window, since the Duke was seated on her left. "I cannot see it very well, but perhaps the view will be clearer on our return."

They journeyed on another half mile. "To the right, you may observe the cross that marks the Pilgrim's Way to the shrine of St Edburg," Monty informed them.

Diana dutifully noted the stone cross.

They travelled by more fields, and Monty could not resist commenting on the nearby flocks. "We now come across some sheep, which I believe are a rare and fascinating breed. Would you not say so, Eastleigh?"

The Duke froze him with a look. Isabella Wilde, not party to the joke, feigned a yawn. "Must you remark upon every hovel and haystack we pass, Mr Chalmers?"

Diana, feeling sorry for Monty at this rudeness, drew from her recent study of ovine husbandry. "I believe their dewlap marks them as Merinos, sir."

Monty, taken aback, was silent for some seconds, then laughed. "I bow to your superior knowledge, madam." There was a twinkle of amusement in his eye. This girl, he decided, would be more than a match for his friend. If Eastleigh didn't make a hash of the whole thing. Which was not beyond him in Monty's opinion.

The coach was the last vehicle to arrive at Abbey Lake. Servants had been sent ahead earlier in the morning, with rugs, chairs, food and other provisions. Frederick's phaeton had unsurprisingly arrived first, with the lighter gig that transported Charles and Lady Julia also preceding.

Diana was glad to step down into the soft green grass of the meadow by the lake. The Duke's proximity and Miss Wilde's hostility had combined to make the journey an ordeal.

Lady Julia, greeting her, twirled a pale lilac parasol. "I declare that Mr Lewis is as reckless a driver as my cousin. I can only suppose that he wished to offload me as soon as possible.

I call it an utter torment."

This was deliberately said in front of the driver in question. Charles grinned. "Since we did not lose a wheel or overturn on a pothole, but were delivered safely to our destination, I call it a great success."

"Did my brother drive at his customary snail's pace?" Lady Julia asked Diana.

"Jenkins drove the coach at a speed judicious for these roads," the Duke replied. He looked at Diana as if for corroboration.

"It was a very comfortable ride," she said, though this was far from the truth in her case.

Lady Julia seized Diana's arm to "show her the lake". But Diana soon discovered that her true purpose was to extol the virtues of Charles Lewis, and to discover anything else that Diana might know about him.

Diana, who had not thought Lady Julia serious in her flirtations with Charles, was alarmed. She did not express this, but she remembered what Charles had said about the Duke rejecting his sister's suitors. *He will accept nothing less than a Marquess.* Charles, for all his virtues, was not that nor ever could be.

"He is the most agreeable and fascinating man I have ever met! Certainly the most intelligent. Tell me all that you know of him, Miss St Clair."

"I am sure that you know as much as I do. He is indeed very agreeable," Diana replied.

Lady Julia cast her a sudden glance. "I suppose that you do not… that you and he…?"

"We have no understanding. We are simply friends," Diana assured her. As she said it, she wondered if she did feel anything more. Certainly she had liked Charles above all other young men she had met. But he did not arouse in her the same kind of feelings as the Duke of Eastleigh did.

As this thought struck her she stopped, horrified. Had she developed feelings for the Duke? O, how foolish she had been if so. And how had she not realised until this moment? The weakness she felt around him, the desire she felt to be near him. How his touch burned her skin and made her long for more of it.

They were shameful feelings, she was sure. All the more so because the Duke had done nothing to provoke them. Diana remembered with unease his condemnation of her at the Cavendish's ball. How badly he would think of her now, if he knew what sensations he inspired in her.

Diana's new self-realisation made her ripe for Isabella Wilde's malice. All smiles and winsome charm, Miss Wilde inveigled Diana to take a turn with her about the lake while the lunch provisions were being set out. Diana would have preferred Lady Julia to accompany them, but she was being instructed in angling by Monty and Charles Lewis.

The two women set off, with Miss Wilde offering various comments on the weather and the scenery until they were both out of earshot and out of sight of the rest of the party. For as they neared the water's edge, they were screened by trees.

It was here that Miss Wilde finally spoke her true purpose. "You will forgive my directness Miss St Clair, but I wished to speak to you on a personal matter."

Diana, more alarmed than intrigued, assured Miss Wilde that her directness did not offend.

"It is for your own sake that I do so. You have become enamoured of His Grace, have you not?"

Shocked, Diana stammered that she was sure she had not.

"Come now, Miss St Clair. You have not acted improperly but you are very young. And sometimes when one is unused to comporting oneself around gentlemen, one does not manage to conceal one's sentiments so well."

Diana tried to protest. "I am sure that I do not... that I have never..."

Miss St Clair interrupted her with a little laugh. "Do not distress yourself. I am sure the Duke is not too irritated. Embarrassed, perhaps. But he is a man of the world and must recognise how young you are."

These words stung all the more, for they were exactly what the Duke had said to Diana the previous evening. It had been pity, then, that she had seen in his eyes. He was sorry for her that she felt as she did and had perhaps meant to issue a gentle caution.

Diana had never felt such wretchedness or such humiliation. It was worse than any time he had glared at her. Worse, even, than when he had rebuked her. Isabella Wilde was the last person from whom Diana would have wanted to seek counsel. But in her anguish, she found herself doing so. "What should I do? Only tell me how I can repair the situation?"

Miss Wilde gave another deprecatory laugh. "There is no need to make a melodrama of it, my dear. Simply refrain from trailing him like a lost lamb. I am sure it will all soon be forgotten."

If Diana had been less disturbed, she would have realised the untruth of this, for she had never followed him about. But her distress made her easy to deceive. "I must thank you, I suppose, for your kindness in alerting me."

The other woman made a dismissive gesture. "It is of no consequence. You should be aware, for an announcement is only a matter of time, that His Grace and I have an understanding. That is why I felt it my place to speak."

"I am very glad for you both," Diana said, trying to mean it.

"Thank you. Our fathers were great friends, and it is something both families have wished for a long time. You are not to be blamed for not knowing, for you do not move in the same circles as we do. Though I am sure I am very glad to have had this opportunity to make your acquaintance."

The sun had gone out of the day for Diana. She did her best to enjoy the picnic and the subsequent entertainments. For those who did not know her so well, her mortification was easy to conceal.

Only the Duke observed that she was subdued. He desired nothing more than to be alone with her but seemed to be thwarted at every attempt.

Before lunch Diana had been commandeered first by his sister and then by Isabella Wilde. After lunch Miss Wilde had attached herself to the Duke in an alarmingly proprietary manner, and by the time he had shaken her off, Diana was being instructed in angling by Monty.

He regarded her now: the slim form in a simple muslin gown, attempting to hold and cast the rod according to Monty's directions. He was on the point of approaching them when Miss Wilde accosted him yet again.

"You are not fond of angling yourself, Your Grace? I dare say it is a very monotonous activity, for the fish seem so rarely to bite."

The Duke, who was very fond of angling, made a non-committal reply. His attention was still fixed on Miss St Clair and his friend.

Isabella Wilde observed this with some irritation. She decided more machinations were in order. Adopting a saccharine tone, she commented on the pair. "What a very sweet young woman Miss St Clair is, and how patient Mr Chalmers is. I am so glad to have made her acquaintance. Her mother, too, is most charming."

"Indeed."

"She is to be congratulated on securing such a good match for her daughter. For it is very suitable, and they must all be very happy."

She had the Duke's attention now. "A good match?"

"Her engagement to Mr Lewis, of course. Though I do not believe it has been publicly announced."

There was a harsh edge to the Duke of Eastleigh's voice. "Miss St Clair is engaged to be married to Mr Lewis?"

"To the best of my knowledge. For I spoke of it with Mrs St Clair only yesterday." Isabella Wilde felt more than justified in her lies, for Charles Lewis would be a far more appropriate match for the St Clair girl than the Duke of Eastleigh. After all the girl was a nobody. Isabella considered that she was saving the Duke from a disastrous error by ending any intentions he had towards her.

Charles Lewis was at that moment in merry conversation with Lady Julia. The Duke had paid less attention than he might have done to this flirtation, being preoccupied with Diana.

"There is some reason that they do not announce it?" the Duke asked.

Isabella gave an airy shrug. "I imagine they plan a long engagement. She is very young, of course."

This was a lucky barb, for Miss Wilde did not know how much this point had troubled the Duke. He felt all the worse for her saying it. He supposed it was not Miss Wilde's fault that she should be the bearer of such ill news, for she was not privy to his thoughts. Nonetheless, he resented her for it. It was with some effort that he remained civil while she chattered away on topics that did not interest him.

An engagement might be broken, the Duke reasoned. All the more so if it were not yet announced. But his heart was heavy. Diana St Clair had displayed no partiality for him. She had even sought to avoid his company that day. He had overstepped yesterday. He ought never to have waltzed with her, let alone taken her out onto the terrace. He could not be accused of any insult to Mr Lewis by doing so, for he had not been aware of their arrangement.

Yet he had doubtless embarrassed Miss St Clair. He would avoid doing so again.

CHAPTER 20

Undaunted by fatigue following the day's activities, Lady Julia demanded that there should be more dancing that evening. "Our friends have spent all day in rehearsal, and I am eager to hear them play."

Diana wanted nothing more than to go to bed. She was not sure she could face the ordeal of watching the Duke dance endlessly with Miss Wilde.

When they dressed for dinner, Diana went into her mother's room to recount more of the day. Mrs St Clair at once perceived that her daughter was not in her usual spirits.

"Something troubles you, my dear? Pray tell me what it is. Are you ill?"

It was all Diana could do not to weep. "O! Mamma. Everything has gone wrong."

It took Mrs St Clair some time to extract the story from her daughter. Much of it made little sense, at least according to what she herself had observed. Diana omitted the accusation that she was enamoured of the Duke, for she could not bear to admit it to her mother or even herself at that moment. She only revealed that her conduct had supposedly annoyed him, and that he was betrothed to Miss Wilde.

"And you received all this information from Miss Wilde?" she asked Diana.

"Yes. She suggested that I had greatly embarrassed the Duke. I can hardly bear to look at him now. I am so ashamed."

"Do not become hysterical, my dear. For what it is worth, I do not think you have exposed yourself. For I observed you myself at the dancing last night. I also did not see anything in His Grace's manner to suggest annoyance on his part." Quite the opposite, but Mrs St Clair did not disclose this to Diana. The situation was already too complicated. She privately suspected that Isabella Wilde's accusation was the result of jealousy. Even if she were engaged to the Duke of Eastleigh, she might yet feel threatened by his paying attention to another woman.

"Are you sure mamma? I hope that you are right."

"I confess I am surprised to learn that he is soon to be engaged to Miss Wilde, but perhaps I should not be. For it is doubtless a very suitable alliance for a man in his position. Miss Wilde's father is a baronet and the younger son of marquess, so Miss Etteridge informs me. You remember, dear, that once you declared you would only marry for love. Consider yourself fortunate that you are free to do so, for Miss Wilde may not have had that choice," Mrs St Clair said.

Diana looked at herself in the glass. She was wan, and her eyes were reddened. "Do you mean that she does not love him?"

"I cannot say, my dear. But dab some of my rosewater on your face and restore your complexion. We will go down to dinner, and all shall be well."

Following a disappointing day, the Duke was having an excruciating evening. Miss Wilde attached herself to him at every opportunity, and he could not shake her.

Even worse, Diana St Clair seemed to be actively avoiding him. When he had spoken to her, she had averted her eyes and appeared anxious for their conversation to end.

Not that the damnable Charles Lewis was paying her any attention. The fellow was entirely absorbed with Julia. The Duke felt a growing irritation as he watched the pair of them. Private engagement or not, it must be humiliating for Miss St Clair to see herself so disregarded.

He would have words with Julia as well. She might not be party to the knowledge of the engagement, but her flirtation with Mr Lewis lacked decorum.

He watched as the pair of them laughed, Julia pretending to fan Mr Lewis with a contraption of peacock feathers that she held.

The Duke felt an urge to punch the man. No wonder Miss St Clair appeared disquieted. How could a fellow have the promise of a woman like that, and treat her so?

Monty was aware of unhappy undercurrents in the room, though he did not know exactly how the stars had become crossed.

"An enjoyable if fatiguing day," he remarked to Eastleigh. "I do not think I shall play cards later. My brain is befogged. An early night will restore my acuity."

The Duke, finding the current scene increasingly less bearable, also desired oblivion. He downed another brandy and signalled to the servant to refill his glass, offering likewise to Monty.

Monty declined. "It's an excellent vintage but I've had my fill. I observe that Miss St Clair is unpartnered. Shall I remedy the situation?"

"I shall go." The Duke stood, making his way over to Diana.

She looked up and there was such sadness in her eyes that it was all he could do not to take her in his arms and hold her.

The Duke kept his manner light. "I see that once again you do not dance. Allow me to claim you for the next measure."

To his surprise and disappointment she declined. "It is very kind of you, sir, but I find that I am quite tired." Across the room she saw Miss Wilde regarding her with unsettling hostility. "I think that Miss Wilde is also without a partner, and I am sure she may be less tired than I am."

The Duke was sure that Diana was not simply tired. She was unhappy, and he could only assume it was due to Charles

Lewis's neglect. With their engagement being a secret that he was not supposed to be privy to, the Duke felt powerless to intervene. Not that he wanted to assist her progress with another man, but he could not bear to see her suffering.

"I am very sorry that you are so fatigued. We should perhaps have chosen an easier trip than the lake," he said.

"O not at all. I found Abbey Lake quite delightful," she assured him.

Unsure of what else to say, the Duke once again fell on his flock. "Tomorrow we will have less strenuous amusements. And I must keep my promise to you and to your mother, regarding my sheep."

The woolly beasts might be good for something other than a roast joint, if they enabled him to finally get her alone.

Isabella Wilde was not satisfied with the progress she was making. She had done well in seeing the St Clair chit off, for the girl was blatantly avoiding the Duke. She appeared to have rebuffed him now, for they did not stand up together to dance, though Isabella was sure it was his motive in approaching her.

The girl looked miserable too. Silly little fool, Isabella thought. She ought to have known her place.

Isabella was confident that whatever Eastleigh's sentiments were towards the girl, he would have done no more than to amuse himself with her. He could not have had any serious intentions towards her. She reasoned that she was saving them both from a dalliance as futile as it was foolish.

Nonetheless, she was irked to be paid so little attention herself. When Julia had asked her down to Eastleigh, mentioning that the Amberforth affair had "come to nothing", Isabella had supposed there would be a speedy transfer of interest in her direction. After all there had been talk of such an alliance some years ago, between the late Duke and her father. Having grown up with the notion that she was fit for a Duke, Isabella Wilde had been choosier with other suitors.

This presumption and its resultant attitude went some way to explaining why, at the age of nearly nine-and-twenty, Miss Wilde remained unmarried. She was not averse to the notion of marital duties, as some women were. Indeed the Duke's apparent vigour, properly managed, might be an advantage rather than a chore. Like any wise female Miss Wilde had safeguarded her maidenhood.

Now she wondered if its yielding might accelerate the achievement of her goal.

Watching Eastleigh mooning after the St Clair girl, drinking far more heavily than he was accustomed to, Isabella Wilde felt encouraged. It might take only a little more wine to bring about a situation that would force his hand.

CHAPTER 21

The Duke had indeed drunk more heavily than his usual habit. As such, he fell into a deep, drugged sleep for the first half of the night. As the hours passed, the amount he had drunk began to have the opposite effect.

He awoke in the early hours before dawn with an urgent bodily need. It was still dark but a pale glow emanated from the windows, which the Duke preferred undraped at this time of year.

He thought at first that his imagination played tricks on him. For there appeared to be something in the bed beside him. A dark form, beneath the bedclothes. Someone. He heard a soft snore and froze. What or who could it be?

In alarm, he peered closer. It appeared to be a woman. He at once recognised the distinct perfume of Isabella Wilde.

Horror began to overtake him. Just how drunk had he been the previous evening? He had absolutely no memory of bringing the woman into his bedchamber, let alone any scene of seduction. He hadn't even desired to do such.

How could he get her out of his bed? To be discovered thus would be fatal. He was already compromised. What if he had ruined her? He would be forced to do the honourable thing.

Monty had been more sober than he had. He might be able to cast some light on the hazy events of the previous evening. The Duke looked again at the sleeping form of Miss Wilde. She seemed to be in a heavy slumber.

Lighting a candle, he pulled a robe around him and went into the corridor, closing the door behind him as softly as he could.

Monty was not pleased to have his own slumber interrupted

by some fool rapping on his door. At first burying his head under his pillow, he was finally unable to ignore it. He raised his head. "Who is it? Surely it's the middle of the damned night?"

"It's Eastleigh," hissed a familiar voice.

Wondering what on earth his friend might want at this hour, Monty groggily arose to open his door. The Duke stood there with a candle.

"What sort of a wretch are you, to drag a fellow up at this hour? There's no fire, is there? Is the house invaded by thieves?"

"Something very awkward has happened. I have awoken to find Miss Wilde in my bed."

For a wild moment Monty thought his friend was joking. Joke or not, he could not help a burst of laughter which the Duke hurriedly shushed.

"There is nothing amusing in the situation, Chalmers. I cannot for the life of me recall how this may have happened. I have no memory of anything other than going to bed, quite alone."

"You are quite sure that you did not admit her in the night? You were throwing back the brandy with some abandon, as I recall."

"I am quite sure. At least I think I am sure. I certainly had no sober desire to admit the woman. How came she there?"

Monty was thinking. He knew Isabella Wilde's hopes - expectations, even - towards Eastleigh. She had displayed a marked dislike of Diana St Clair, even being openly disdainful towards the girl. Eastleigh had not been as guarded as he supposed in concealing his sentiments towards the young woman.

Had Miss Wilde contrived some devilish plan to settle the situation for once and for all? Monty would not put it past her. "This is a pretty pickle, indeed."

"It is more serious than a pickle, Chalmers. What in the world am I to do?"

Monty thought for a moment. "Let us suppose that Miss Wilde has been sleepwalking. Inadvertently she found her way into your bedchamber. That seems a possible explanation."

Possible or not, and frankly it was highly implausible, it did not absolve the Duke from having to save her reputation, which he pointed out.

"I think it may be said that Miss Wilde might not be adverse to you offering to save her honour. However, I find myself questioning whether she would so readily accept the same courtesy from me," Monty said.

The Duke was losing patience. "Come to the point, for heaven's sake. She may wake at any time!"

"What I propose is an exchange. You spend the rest of the night here, and I will take your place in your room. For I think that given a choice between my offer of matrimony, and a suggestion that the entire affair is hushed up, the lady will opt for the latter."

"And if she does not?"

"I will find some means of escape. I may produce an earlier wife, perhaps. Or flee abroad."

The Duke was silent. "This is an enormous favour you do me, Chalmers."

"Think nothing of it. You might rise early and find some way to prevent your servant from attending you at the usual hour. Otherwise I fear they may be shocked to discover not one but two unexpected inhabitants."

This plan was put into action. The Duke stayed in Monty's room. His friend slipped off and apparently took his place without rousing Miss Wilde, for no screams of horror or running footsteps were heard. The Duke could not sleep another wink, and sat by the window, waiting for dawn to fully lighten the sky and bring an end to the ordeal.

A loud shriek woke Monty from a very pleasant dream featuring a winning hand of cards and an accommodating Frenchwoman *en déshabillé*.

"What are you doing here?!"

Monty opened his eyes. No winsome French dame but a horrified Miss Wilde was glaring down at him. She clutched the bedclothes against her in the manner of a shield.

Monty remained composed. "I might well ask you the same, madam."

"O!" Miss Wilde was too furious for further speech.

Monty exited the bed and stood with his back to Miss Wilde, as a show of deference to her modesty. "We seem to be in a puzzling predicament." His tone was amused, but his bedmate's was not.

"You have… you have outraged me, sir! You have ruined me!"

Monty turned back to face her. "I think not, since my breeches are still intact."

"O!"

Isabella Wilde was simultaneously enraged and mystified. How had this happened? She could have sworn it was the Duke of Eastleigh whose powerful form she had slipped into bed next to. He had been so deeply asleep that she had decided there was no need to wake him and sacrifice her virtue. They would both be compromised enough when the servant arrived to wake them the next morning.

But no servant had yet come, and here she was in bed with Montague Chalmers!

Somehow she had been double crossed. A substitution had taken place, and her plan was foiled. More than that, she realised that the Duke had effectively repudiated her. He might have simply extracted himself and spent the night playing cards or doing some activity where he could be witnessed to have been alone, saving her honour.

Instead he had sent another man to take his place in bed with her.

Isabella Wilde knew the nightmarish situation she was now in was of her own making, but that only made it worse. She had thrown away her good reputation for nothing. Bleakly she looked up at Monty. "What can we do?"

Monty took pity on her. She had gambled with high stakes and lost, but he could prevent her total ruin. "The wine was heavy last night, following a fatiguing day. Such circumstances, I believe, may be conducive to somnambulance."

"Sleepwalking?" Her tone held incredulity.

"Quite so. A strange coincidence, perhaps, that we should both have made our unconscious way here. But it seems the likeliest explanation, in my view."

She ought to be grateful, she knew. Montague Chalmers was offering her a way out. She gritted her teeth. "It would seem so. Yet I do not think we need call a physician, do you?"

"Most certainly not. Not where there is sure to be a swift recovery. I feel myself already well recovered, so shall depart. Once you are also recovered, you may do likewise. For I don't think the servant will attend at this early hour."

This was said to reassure her. But it was all the more galling for Isabella Wilde. For she realised that the two men had conspired together to devise this subterfuge and keep the servant away.

After Monty had gone, she left for her own room, treading lightly and swiftly down the corridor. It would not do for anyone else in the household to be awoken.

Monty reached his own room, where an anxious Eastleigh awaited him.

"What has happened? She is gone?"

Monty gave him a brief rundown of events. "The lady was

not entirely happy to discover me in your bed. But we came to an understanding."

"An understanding? You have not proposed marriage to the woman?" the Duke asked, alarmed.

"Not at all. An understanding of mutual discretion." Monty smiled with satisfaction.

Eastleigh expressed his deep gratitude. "I cannot say I relish the prospect of encountering her at breakfast."

His friend allayed this concern. "I shouldn't think you will have to. Some feminine complaint will no doubt prevent her from joining the rest of the company. I predict she will then arrange for her carriage, and we shall see her no more."

"I hope you are right. It is a very regrettable business," the Duke said.

"But a business that is over and dealt with. Leaving the field clear to pursue the delightful Miss St Clair."

Eastleigh, who had been regarding his grounds as dawn brightened them, swung around. "I beg your pardon?"

"That lovely young woman by whom you are clearly more attracted than you ever were by Miss Wilde," Monty said. Given his role in remedying the previous night's affair, he felt entitled to amuse himself now.

"I have no intentions towards Miss St Clair or any other woman," the Duke asserted. "Besides," he added, giving himself away, "she is engaged to Mr Lewis."

This was news to Monty. "Is she? By Jove, that does surprise me. I would have wagered him for a brother-in-law over a rival any day." As soon as he had said it he regretted it, for he did not want to cause trouble for Julia. "I speak out of turn. Forgive me."

But the Duke's concentration was on his earlier comment. "Why should it surprise you? They were acquainted before they came here. It is undoubtedly a very suitable match."

Except for Charles Lewis's attention being solely focused on

Lady Julia, Monty thought though he said nothing.

Returning to his own room, the Duke now considered the second part of Monty's comment. Things were clearly going too far with his sister and Lewis. He would need to have words with her.

CHAPTER 22

O ver breakfast, at which Miss Wilde was fortunately absent, the Duke announced his plans to show the St Clairs his sheep that morning.

Lady Julia merely raised her eyebrows and exchanged a glance with Monty. The Misses Selcome, who were not privy to the sheep ruse, were unperturbed. Mr Ravenscroft, not privy either, asked Mrs St Clair if she had a fondness for the animals.

It was all Julia could do to keep a straight face at this. Her attempts to conceal her mirth as a fit of choking earned her a glare from her brother.

"We own a flock of Cotswold Longhorns," Mrs St Clair told Mr Ravenscroft. She kept her composure, though she was not entirely at ease. She was quite sure by now that the Duke did not have a particular interest in sheep, but she was uncertain as to what his intentions towards her daughter were.

"I have heard of them, a rare breed, I believe? Has your family long been in sheep farming?" Mr Ravenscroft asked.

"We have not. The sheep were an unusual bequest. Due to our inexperience in their husbandry, His Grace has kindly offered to provide us with guidance." Mrs St Clair managed to make it sound the most natural thing in the world that a duke should exchange information on sheep farming with her, and the topic of conversation soon changed.

Shortly after breakfast, the Duke drove Mrs St Clair and Diana over the Eastleigh estate. Despite Miss Wilde's warning to her, Diana could not help but feel happy to be spending this time with him. After all, the outing was innocent enough and Miss Wilde was indisposed that day anyway. For this reason she had not been at breakfast and had not been very much missed by anyone.

The St Clairs were an appreciative audience when it came to the many features of the estate. Diana had spent most of her life in a small village and genuinely liked the countryside as much as she liked town. She was not fazed by country roads or the sight and scent of livestock. She was used to walking through fields and lanes, for when one does not own a carriage, there is little choice about doing so.

Where another woman might have been dismayed to get mud on her hem as she stepped down from a carriage, Diana was untroubled. She managed as gracefully as she could, knowing from experience that a few clods of earth were not the ruination of a gown. Mud was certainly easier to launder than grease from a carriage wheel or spilt wine.

The Duke found her enthusiastic and unaffected, and his admiration for her grew.

"What pretty black and white markings these sheep have!" Diana said, as they drew up at one field.

"They are Welsh Hill sheep," the Duke told her, having discovered this from his land steward the previous day. "The ewes have not yet lambed. If your own property can accommodate, I hope you will permit me to make you a gift of some lambs once they do."

"They are very picturesque," Mrs St Clair said, thanking him. "It would be very generous of you, Your Grace."

They drove past one of the tenant farmhouses and the Duke stopped to address a few words to the farmer. He knew the man by name and they seemed to be on congenial terms.

A small girl in a pale blue frock and apron ran out and tugged at the man's arm. She whispered something to him. The farmer chuckled.

"The barn cat, Bessie, had another litter a few days past. Our Lizzie wonders if the ladies would like to see the kittens?

Very proud of them, is Lizzie."

The Duke turned to Diana. She expressed eagerness to see them, as much for the little girl's sake as for her own.

"If you would care to step down, Miss St Clair, the ground is quite dry." The Duke extended his hand to Diana, helping her alight. She tripped and might have stumbled against him but managed to recover herself. It brought to mind that other disastrous occasion when she had collided with him and she felt her face redden and could not look at him.

Mrs St Clair would have been content to remain in the carriage, but like Diana she did not want to disappoint the child. The Duke helped her down as well. The three of them, accompanied by the farmer's small daughter, made their way across the dried mud of the yard and around the side of the farmhouse. Here, by the barn, was a tumbledown sty half curtained by nettles. The child knelt down and reached inside, bringing out a tiny grey kitten, which she presented to Diana.

Diana clasped the animal as it mewed loudly. "The darling little thing! I should think it is terrified to be away from its mother," she said, as she petted it.

The Duke stood there in silence, watching the pair of them. He held his hands behind his back, his tall, distinguished figure contrasting with the slender frame of the young woman.

Mrs St Clair regarded them both. The Duke's expression was unmistakeable as he gazed at Diana. He was clearly in love with her. Mrs St Clair wondered where it all might end. She ought to have been flattered on behalf of her daughter, to have such a great man pay her his attentions.

Instead she felt as anxious as the mother cat, who now emerged from the sty yowling loudly for the return of her offspring. Diana gave a last embrace to the kitten and handed it gently back to Lizzie, who restored it to its mother. She picked up the kitten in her mouth and slunk back inside the den.

The Duke gave a coin to the little girl as they left, promising her father that his steward would inspect some fencing that needed repairs. "We must rebuild that sty as well, once it is no longer in use as a nursery."

Diana could not remember enjoying a morning so much. The Duke was very courteous to both her mother and herself. He showed them different aspects of Eastleigh and its land. Everything they viewed was well-built and maintained, and where it was not, the Duke remarked upon it and committed it to his memory to inform his steward.

They drove as far as the top of the small hill which had been rejected as a picnic spot. From here the view of the house and across the surrounding countryside was magnificent. Mrs St Clair remarked on its splendour, but the Duke's reply held only humility. "My family is very privileged to have this land entrusted to us. I hope I do not sound excessively proud to say that I believe it some of the finest country in England."

"Seen from this aspect, on this fine morning, it would be difficult to find argument with that, Your Grace."

The Duke turned to Diana. "And what do you think, Miss St Clair?" His voice was softer as he spoke to her.

"I think it is the most beautiful view I have ever seen. And I am very grateful to you for having shown it to us," Diana said. She was regarding the panoramic vista as she spoke, and the Duke was gazing at her.

"I hope that this will not be the last time you see it," he said.

Diana turned to him, her eyes shining. She said nothing, but something passed between them. Again she felt that compelling desire to remain in his presence. Simply to be with him.

The Duke was now half grateful, half regretful that Mrs St Clair had accompanied them. For without her chaperonage, he was not sure that he could have resisted giving in to his baser urges. He had a vision of Diana laid down before him in the soft grass, as he made love to her in the open air.

It could not go on. He was going out of his mind. Lewis or not, the Duke was determined to stake his claim.

When they arrived back at the house and stepped down from the carriage, the Duke suggested they might like to see the rose garden since there was still some time before lunch. "We have many early roses, that are already in bloom."

Mrs St Clair, aware of his true aspiration, excused herself. "It has been a very pleasurable outing, but I hope you will forgive me if I return to my room to rest. I am sure Diana would be delighted to see it."

The Duke wished her well, and led Diana to the rose garden, which was sheltered on three sides by tall yew hedges. There was already an abundance of blooms, from roses that climbed over an arched pergola to bushes and sprays of flowers.

"June is said to be the best month for roses, but the sheltered and sunny aspect here encourages early flowering," the Duke said.

"It is very beautiful," Diana agreed.

"My mother loved roses and arranged much of the layout and choice of plants. She had the pergolas built, though the stone bench in the centre is an older feature. We may sit for a while, if you would like?"

Diana was both nervous and excited to be alone with the Duke. She tried to remain composed and not to reveal her apprehension. The Duke spoke of his boyhood, where it related to the garden and trees he had climbed, and various boyish escapades. He sat next to her on the bench but they were not as in such close proximity as they had been in the carriage. Still, she was very much aware of his presence.

"You grew up in Gloucestershire I believe, Miss St Clair?"

"I did. At first we lived not far from Cheltenham. After my father's death some years ago we moved to a village named Didmarton, near the border with Wiltshire," she told him.

The Duke knew of the St Clairs' altered circumstances following the death of Rainault St Clair. "I am sorry that you were not able to stay in your family home."

"It is kind of you to say so, sir, but I do not know that my mother minded so much. It was in great need of repair and was not as comfortable as it might have been. We were quite happy in Didmarton." This was far from the truth, for they had been lean and difficult years.

"Lady Cavendish mentioned to me that you assisted your mother in business matters. You must have been very young to do so."

"There was no one else who might have assisted us, and I found it interesting," Diana said.

The Duke regarded her. He wondered how attached to Charles Lewis she was, and whether that attachment might be broken. If he had the chance to spend more time with her, might he win her affection himself? Once or twice when she had looked at him, he had felt that she liked him. Some women would be attracted by his titles alone, but he sensed that she was not one of them.

He knew now that he wanted a full and proper marriage, not just a wife in name. The near disaster with Lady Jane Amberforth had taught him that. He wanted a woman who might be a companion, a partner and a lover. Could a girl as young and beautiful as Diana ever feel the same desire for him that he felt for her? He had a powerful urge to embrace her and find out.

As he thought this, his eyes on her lips, he perceived that she trembled. At once he was concerned. "You feel the cold, Miss St Clair?"

"No, sir. It is only… I do not know what it is. The weather is quite warm." Her eyes met his and the Duke felt that same connection with her that he had done on the hillside.

Unable to resist, he moved his hand to her face, cupping her chin, his thumb brushing over her mouth. She gave a slight gasp and her lips parted.

But she did not resist. She remained there, still gazing into his eyes.

He tilted her face upwards and leant down, bringing his mouth down upon hers. He felt her start, then relax. He brought his other hand around to support her head, clasping her towards him in his embrace. As his lips moved hers apart, she once again stiffened slightly. But as he continued to taste her, entwining with her, she seemed to melt into him.

His hand moved down to her waist, his thumb brushing the side of her breast through her gown. It was wrong, he knew, and he was a scoundrel to be treating a maiden in such a way, but he felt as though he were drowning.

As he caressed her she arched against him, and he knew that she was capable of desire. This knowledge only inflamed him.

He had to break away. It took every effort of will, and he felt a physical pain in doing so, but he broke off the embrace. They were both silent for a moment, absorbing what had just transpired.

"Forgive me, Miss St Clair. I fear the heady scent of the roses overcame me. I did not intend to misuse you in this manner."

He looked as contrite as he had done when making his earlier apology to her. "It is quite alright, Your Grace. I believe I was also overcome," Diana said.

Her acknowledgement of her mutual part in their embrace struck him. Most women would have accepted a man's assumption of all blame, but she did not. He attributed it to her youth and inexperience, though her sincerity still moved him.

"We must return to the house, my dear," he said, feeling suddenly very much older. "But I would speak with you again, at another time."

CHAPTER 23

They re-entered the house to find its inhabitants buzzing with the news that Miss Wilde had suddenly and mysteriously departed, along with her maid. She had left without any farewells, and without anyone realising she had gone. Diana was at first horrified that Miss Wild might have witnessed the events in the rose garden. But she soon understood that the other woman had departed several hours before.

"Her maid mentioned to one of the footmen that her mistress had been given news of some emergency, but I do not see how," Lady Julia said. "For there was no post nor any messenger by that hour."

Laura Selcome suggested that Miss Wilde may have been taken ill.

"If so my brother would have called a physician. If she were seriously ill, she would not want to take a long journey by carriage. It is a mystery," Lady Julia remarked.

Various other theories were proposed. Charles Lewis pretended to believe that he thought Miss Wilde had been frightened by a phantom. "A house such as this must surely be haunted. I only wonder if it is one of your wicked ancestors, Lady Julia, or a tragic bride shut into an oak chest."

Julia shivered with horror. "I have never liked that legend. There is a very large chest in my room, and as a child I was always terrified lest I hear the lid creak open in the night."

The matter might have been dropped, for Miss Wilde was not well liked nor very much missed, were it not for the indiscretion of Mr Tanqueray. It was after lunch, when he and the Honourable Frederick were studying some hunting prints at the far end of the drawing room, while the ladies sat at the window end in separate conversation. The other gentleman were all elsewhere, and Mrs St Clair and Miss Etteridge had temporarily retired to their rooms.

Mr Henry Tanqueray had a voice best described, even in its lowest tones, as braying. His conversation with Frederick carried across the room, though little of it was worth overhearing.

"It's a rum thing this Miss Wilde woman vanishing," Mr Tanqueray remarked to his friend. "Only I happened to be outside my room quite late last night, and I'll swear I saw the lady enter Eastleigh's chamber."

All the women pricked up their ears at this, though they made every effort to appear as though they were not doing so.

"Dashed odd, so I thought. Tripping about the corridors in the middle of the night," Mr Tanqueray added.

At the other end of the room, the Misses Selcome did their best to be tactful. Lydia Selcome began to speak, in hurried and loud tones, of a concert she had been to in London.

Laura Selcome also joined in her sister's attempts to provide light conversation. She began a description of the costumes at a masked ball she had been to.

Unfortunately this resulted in both sisters speaking over one another, after which another awkward silence fell.

It was Lady Julia who broke it. "It is no use pretending, for we all heard. I am sure there is any number of explanations."

No one could immediately think of any. The Selcomes rushed to reassure her. "Of course! Of course, my dear. No one in their right mind could suspect anything ill of His Grace. He is all decorum," Laura said.

"Mr Tanqueray was very much 'in his cups', as I believe the expression is, yesterday evening," Lydia added. "Let us not place too much credence in his account. For in a dark house, at night, such things are easily imagined."

Diana remained silent. She could not bring herself to speak. She had been confused ever since the Duke had kissed her and wondered what it might mean.

Now she was doubly shocked by Mr Tanqueray's revelation. The Duke and Miss Wilde were more or less engaged of course. And that state perhaps permitted more liberal intimacy between a couple. But for him to spend the night with Miss Wilde, and then kiss Diana in the rose garden, and then for Miss Wilde to have mysteriously disappeared, it was all too much. What reason could be found that did not reflect terribly on the Duke?

Diana also knew that she had no right to mind about him having another woman in his bedroom. But she did mind, quite bitterly.

Later that day the Duke, unwitting of Mr Tanqueray's revelation, went into the library to fetch a book. It was an hour or so before dinner.

The scene that met his eyes did not please him. Miss Etteridge dozed in a chair, while his sister and Charles Lewis, who had been sitting in close proximity, noticeably moved apart as Charles stood up. The Duke fancied he saw a trace of guilt on their faces.

He greeted them with the usual courtesy, and calmly said that he would like to speak to his sister for a moment. Charles made as if to leave, but the Duke stayed him. "We will talk in my study."

They went to that room, where the Duke at once challenged his sister. "Exactly what do you mean by your behaviour with Mr Lewis?"

It was the wrong approach to take, for Julia's chin tilted and she adopted an air of defiance. "I am not sure that it is any of your concern."

"It is very much my concern, when you are under my

charge, and Mr Lewis is a guest in my home." The Duke stood with his hands folded behind his back, a figure of authority.

Julia resented this even more, for she hated being under guardianship. "There is still nothing for you to work yourself up about. Miss Etteridge was present all the while."

"Miss Etteridge was fast asleep, as you well know. It is ignoble to take advantage of her state. And only think of the distress that your conduct causes to Miss St Clair."

The mention of this name surprised his sister. "Miss St Clair? Why should it have anything to do with her?"

The Duke supposed Julia could not be blamed for ignorance of a secret engagement. But if she were ignorant, then Mr Lewis's conduct was all the more reprehensible for deceiving both women. "She is engaged to Mr Lewis," he told her.

Julia laughed in denial. "No, she is not. He is not engaged to anyone."

"It is a private arrangement, not yet made official. Due, I believe, to her young age."

His sister refuted it once again. She picked up a miniature in a silver frame and studied it idly. "I don't know where you got this notion, James, but it is not true. For I asked Miss St Clair myself."

"You asked her? When was this?" the Duke asked.

"At the lake," Julia told him, putting the portrait down. "I asked if they had an understanding, for I was aware they had a prior acquaintance and seemed to be friends. She assured me that they did not. Do you really think so ill of me, that I should openly flirt with another woman's betrothed?"

"You admit that you flirt, then?"

Exasperation rose. "For heaven's sake, why should I not? There is no harm in it. Do you expect me to live as though I were in a nunnery?"

"I expect you to comport yourself with more decorum," the Duke stated.

This only made his sister more furious. "Then you might like to read about beans and logs in your bible. And removing them from your own eyes, or whatever the text is."

"I beg your pardon?" He was growing as angry as he was bewildered.

"At least I do not welcome nightly visitors to my bedchamber." As soon as she said it, Julia realised she had gone too far. She expected her brother to erupt with rage.

Instead, he grew pale. "What do you mean by this?"

Feeling remorseful, she tried to play it down. "It is nothing. Just something foolish and doubtless untrue that Mr Tanqueray bleated out. I expect he was only jesting."

The Duke felt a heavy weight descend upon him. "You had better tell me what was said."

Reluctantly, Julia revealed it. "He said that he saw a certain lady enter your bedchamber late last night. A lady who is no longer with us. He did not mean to be overheard, he was speaking with Frederick. But you know how his voice carries."

"Who else heard him?"

Julia wished she had never lost her temper, for she saw how agitated her brother was. "Everyone in the room. But no one believed it. I am sure they did not. Or they thought there was some unfortunate misunderstanding. Laura Selcome did not credit it, and Lydia supposed that Mr Tanqueray had been too drunk to know what he saw."

"And Miss St Clair?"

"I have no idea. I am sure she did not believe it either," Julia assured him.

"Miss St Clair said nothing on the matter?" the Duke persisted.

"She did not. Why should it matter so very much if she did? O!" Julia paused, finally reading the truth on her brother's face. "You are in love with her! I ought to have realised. I had supposed you invited them here as some sort of favour to Lady

Cavendish. I am very sorry I invited Miss Wilde down at all then, for all the trouble it has caused. Only I thought you had a fondness for her."

The Duke was in no mood to discuss his love interests with his sister. "My private affairs are not your concern. I would thank you not to meddle in future."

Julia could see that he was both hurt and worried that a slander was being spread about him, which had reached the ears of one he cared about. "You need not worry, James. You must forgive me. I felt angry at your interference and had not intended to do anything except forget the matter. For I know that it is untrue."

"It is not untrue, I am afraid, yet it is also not the situation that you think it is. Mr Chalmers may bear witness on my behalf. But enough damage has been done. I would be grateful if you would not speak of it anymore, to anyone."

Julia acquiesced. "Of course." Then she looked her brother in the eye. "I should tell you that I like Mr Lewis very much. More so than any other gentleman I have ever met. I know he is not titled, but I beg you to at least give him fair consideration."

"Are you telling me that he has proposed to you?" the Duke asked.

"No. But if he did - well - I think I should seriously contemplate accepting him. I would rather be happy, James, than have a lofty title or an ancient coat of arms. And I think it is the same for you, albeit you remain the Duke of Eastleigh regardless."

Chapter 24

Diana and her mother spoke again that evening before dinner. They had not yet had an opportunity to discuss the day's activities. For lunch had been served when they returned, and afterwards Diana had spent the afternoon with the other young ladies.

Now Mrs St Clair remarked on how enjoyable it had been to be given a tour of the Eastleigh estate, and how generous the Duke was in giving them his time. As she spoke, she carefully studied her daughter. She was as certain as she could be that Diana was in love with their host, and she had no doubt that he was enamoured of her.

But she did not see the reaction she had expected in Diana's face. Instead, she looked dejected and troubled.

"It was very kind of him to show us his land," Diana said. Her voice was listless.

"This morning you seemed quite delighted by it all. What ails you now?"

Diana sat in a chair in the corner of the room. "It is something I heard. And I do not know what to think. Nor if I should repeat it."

"It concerns the Duke, perhaps?" This was an easy deduction for her mother.

"Yes. But - O! I do not know!" Diana covered her face, ashamed to even be thinking of it. "I know that they have an understanding, that there was to be an announcement of their betrothal. But from the way he was today, I dared believe for a moment… And now, I do not know what to think." She did not dare tell her mother what had happened in the rose garden.

"You speak of the Duke and Miss Wilde, I presume?" Mrs

St Clair asked.

"I do. She was observed going into his bedroom late last night. And then this morning she is gone - so suddenly! It is all so odd and so unfortunate."

Mrs St Clair could not disagree. Her mind struggled to find some explanation for it, but it looked bleak. For the obvious implication was that the Duke had used Miss Wilde very badly: first entertaining her in his chamber and then casting her out. Or at least insulting her in some manner resulting in her departure.

It did not accord with the impression that Mrs St Clair had developed of the Duke of Eastleigh. Not of his character nor his conduct. The easiest explanation was that Mr Tanqueray was simply mistaken, and she suggested this to her daughter.

"It is what I hope above all else, Mamma. But that does not stop people talking and thinking the worst. Though I am trying not to. I cannot think how he could do anything dastardly and then be so charming to us as he was. For I am sure that he is a very noble man."

Diana's distress was clear, and Mrs St Clair's own discomfort was scarcely less. The situation was already problematic, for if the Duke were engaged to Miss Wilde, his attentions to Diana must be considered suspect. If he had genuine intentions towards Diana, then he must jilt Miss Wilde.

For Diana to be here throughout such an episode was harmful enough.

But for her to be here amid a scandal, known by several of the guests and likely later by all of them was intolerable. For Mrs St Clair knew how rumours spread.

"I am not entirely sure what we should do. But I am of the opinion that it might be wisest for us to return to Somerset. For the Duke may wish for privacy at a time like this. The purported reason for our visit, to view his sheep, has been fulfilled. I do not think there is any discourtesy in us leaving, for I know that Mr Ravenscroft is returning to London tomorrow. It may be convenient for us to share his coach as far as Abingdon, after which we will make our own arrangements."

Diana was close to weeping. "I cannot bear to leave and yet I cannot bear to stay, Mamma. I do not know what has come over me, for I have always found myself capable of maintaining my composure."

Mrs St Clair knew perfectly well what had come over her daughter and was pained to see her suffering.

"All shall be well, my dear. When we are home and have time and peace in which to contemplate matters, everything will become much clearer."

"Are you sure?"

"I am quite sure. Now dry your eyes, and I will inform Jenny of our plans. It is fortunate that Mr Ravenscroft does not have a manservant with him, for it would complicate the matter of the carriage. But we shall be four, and our luggage is not excessive. There is a very fine coaching inn at Abingdon, so Miss Etteridge has mentioned to me, and we shall be very well accommodated."

A focus on these practical issues did much to restore Diana. She repaired her face and hair and chose a gown for dinner. Jenny was tasked with packing and confessed herself glad to be returning to Orchard House. "For it is very grand here, Miss St Clair, but it is not so comfortable or homely."

Dinner that night did not have the same relaxed and convivial atmosphere that there had been on previous evenings. Miss Etteridge, whose superstition concerning the number thirteen had been assuaged by Miss Wilde's departure, joined them. But it was not her presence that dampened the mood.

The Duke of Eastleigh was conscious of the discussions that must have been taking place regarding his night-time activities. It was an effort to play the congenial host. Mrs St Clair, on his left, talked quite normally but he was sure that she must know.

He had been tempted to have Diana seated on the other side of him but realised this would be injudicious. He must halt his plans towards her now, for it would be perceived as very ill if he were thought to have jumped straight from one woman to another.

He wished there were some way the matter might be cleared up. But to do so might only make things worse. For after all, he had allowed Monty to enter his bed in his place, something which could not be disclosed. The interpretation that might be put on that was unthinkable. People might conclude that the two of them had used Miss Wilde, one after the other, and then cast her out.

At the time it had seemed like the only possible course of action but the Duke now regretted it, though he did not know what else could have been done. For even had he simply absented himself and spent the night in his study with a servant to bear witness, the mere fact of Miss Wilde waking in his bed would have been enough to force his hand.

With Monty there, her hand was forced. It had been devious, even if no less devious than the Duke suspected the lady's intentions to have been. But this brought him little comfort.

Diana was again seated by Mr Ravenscroft with Charles Lewis on her other side. She felt that out of all the guests present, these two men were safest. For they had not been there when Mr Tanqueray had blurted out his devastating claim. She might talk normally to them both, with no awkward pauses when each might be thinking of their host and Miss Wilde, and what might have happened.

Mrs St Clair had told Lady Julia of their plans to depart on the morrow, for her to convey to her brother. Lady Julia was genuinely sorry and troubled by their departure, though she guessed what the cause might be. As such she offered no objections nor protestations that they should extend their stay.

"I do hope you will visit us again, and soon. For I know my brother has been delighted to show you Eastleigh, as I have I been to meet you both. And of course there are the sheep," she had said, with a slight smile to Mrs St Clair.

Mrs St Clair had smiled in return. She knew that Lady Julia had become aware of the growing attachment between Diana and His Grace and was indicating that she was not opposed to it. "We have greatly enjoyed our stay," she had replied, "but as you mention it, there is our own flock to consider."

Now Mrs St Clair observed Lady Julia, seated on the other side of Charles Lewis. The girl's behaviour was markedly less flirtatious that evening. Mrs St Clair did not think it was the presence of her companion that constrained her. Lady Julia was not her usual self, and the reason was clear: this awkward rumour concerning her brother.

Lady Julia was also blaming herself for the situation. She was the one who had invited Miss Wilde to Eastleigh. And she could not claim her motive had been entirely altruistic. For although she had genuinely believed her brother admired Isabella Wilde, it was primarily for her own benefit that she wanted him distracted.

Instead it had all gone horribly wrong. The St Clairs were leaving, so that was probably ruined too. If there had even been a chance of anything. Julia had been so wrapped up with Charles Lewis that she had barely noticed the interaction between her brother and Diana St Clair and knew not how things stood. Now she regretted not being more observant and perhaps having been able to better remedy the situation.

The Duke of Eastleigh was disappointed but not wholly

surprised that Mrs St Clair and Diana planned to depart the next day. He tried to tell himself that it was probably for the best. Despite her encouraging response to his embrace he did not know whether she cared for him, for he had assumed her to have feelings for Charles Lewis. He also remained conscious of his age and hers. The damned Ponsonbys were never far from his mind. He had no desire to be a similar laughing stock.

These were his only consolations when a regretful Julia told him the news. "They did not give a reason. Only to say that they had been delighted by Eastleigh but did not wish to trespass on your hospitality overly long."

"I see," the Duke replied.

"I know what you must be thinking," Julia burst out. "That it is all my fault, for I asked Miss Wilde here. And I cannot tell you how sorry I am that I did."

"Calm yourself. I do not in any way blame you. You were not to know that Miss Wilde suffers from sleepwalking," her brother reassured her.

Julia looked incredulous. "Sleepwalking?" Then realisation dawned. "Ah! I see. Then that is how… Well, I am not sure that I fully understand, but if what I now half-suspect is so, then she is a very wicked woman. And you are very lucky to have escaped her, though I am sure I have not the slightest idea how you did it. Nor will you tell me, I suspect?"

"That last suspicion of yours is entirely correct," the Duke said.

"The former too, I don't doubt. But at least she is gone. And a very good riddance to her. I should have hated her for a sister-in-law. Miss St Clair, I should not mind at all. She is a very sweet girl."

"Your approval is appreciated, but misplaced. For I have no imminent plans to provide you with any kind of sister-in-law," her brother told her.

"Then I am very sorry. For I know you like her, and I cannot imagine that she does not feel likewise. For though you frequently infuriate me, I cannot think that any man would make a finer husband than you."

The Duke was touched. "Thank you. But I am afraid your view is not universally held."

Certainly it did not seem that Lady Julia's opinion was shared by Miss St Clair. When she and her mother took their leave the next day, Diana appeared withdrawn. She was courteous and polite, but it was left to Mrs St Clair to make the majority of the farewells.

"We have been quite delighted by Eastleigh and are very grateful that you have invited us here," Mrs St Clair said.

"Not at all. It has been our pleasure to receive you both. I sincerely hope that you will find the occasion to visit again," the Duke said.

Lady Julia agreed. "I hope I may call on you when I am next in Bath. For I understand that you reside only just outside the city."

"We do. And we would be very glad to see you at any time," Mrs St Clair said, doubting such a visit would ever materialise. But these were the conventional things one said at such a time.

The Duke tried not to keep looking at Diana. He wanted to memorise every aspect of her features, even the sadness on them today. If her sadness were due to leaving Eastleigh, that was at least something. But despite Julia's reassurance, he still feared Diana's distress was over Charles Lewis.

Mr Ravenscroft also took his leave, and the four passengers ascended into the carriage.

The Duke watched it until it had travelled past the curve of the driveway and out of sight, and returned inside to attend to his remaining guests.

CHAPTER 25

Being back at Orchard House was a tonic for Diana. She was not quite restored to her old self, but she did what she could to keep busy. Although there were ample funds for servants now, certain tasks were a hard habit to break.

Fortunately there was plenty to occupy herself with. Building was nearly complete on the new croft house and there was a need to arrange its furnishing. It was decided some hens should be purchased, and a coop set up in the orchard. Then there were the sheep which were now lambing.

One lamb was rejected by its mother and Tom brought it to the house. He nodded towards the stove and Diana first feared that he meant them to roast it. She eventually established that it needed to be kept warm and fed milk every few hours. She did this, and when another ewe had a stillbirth, Tom coaxed the sheep to take the rejected lamb.

Diana tried not to think about the Duke of Eastleigh. It was hard, for the more she tried to put him out of her mind, the more she dreamt of him. His dark, flawlessly handsome features. The height and strength of his body. The firm warmth of his lips as he had kissed her. She had heard nothing more from him and feared he had simply been toying with her. She saw no announcement of his betrothal or marriage in the newspaper but thought it must surely only be a matter of time.

Maria and Henrietta returned from Wells, full of news about the people they had met and their activities there. They also brought gifts for Diana who celebrated her eighteenth birthday at the start of July.

"Wells is a very fine city, not on the scale of Bath, of course," Maria said. "But we met some very fine people, and Miss

Beasley and Mrs Petersham were all kindness."

"Do they both still live there, now Mrs Petersham is married?" Mrs St Clair asked.

"Indeed. She and her husband have a house just two streets away from the Beasleys' home. It is all very convenient. But tell us more of Eastleigh. Is the house very grand?" Maria asked.

This was addressed to Diana, who confirmed that it was. "It is very ancient, or parts of it are. And it is not modernised upstairs, though the salons are in a more recent fashion. The dining room, also."

Maria was uninterested in these details. "And what of the Duke? And his sister? Is she truly as much a tearaway as her reputation?"

"Not at all. I found her very agreeable," Diana said.

"And the Duke?" Henrietta prompted. She was making some small repairs to a gown, claiming that the maid "did not have a sufficiently delicate touch". Diana suspected that her sister simply missed the needlework she had been used to doing. For Henrietta was very skilled at embroidery.

"The Duke was a very gracious host," Diana told her.

Henrietta was scornful. "La! That means nothing at all. Tell us what he was really like. For you cannot have spent days and nights under his roof without forming some better picture of him."

Diana wished her mother was with them for she might have redirected the conversation. But Mrs St Clair was in the garden at that moment. "You have seen him yourself, so I need not describe his appearance to you. He is courteous to his guests and very generous, and his servants respect and like him."

"He sounds a paragon," Maria said. "I thought he looked very haughty when we glimpsed him in Bath. He never danced when he attended the assemblies. I suppose he is one of those objectionable men who never dances, regarding it as an activity below their contempt."

Diana was forced to defend the Duke. "That is not so in his case, for he dances very well. We had dancing at Eastleigh on more than one evening, though we were not a large party."

She had her sisters' attention now. "You are not telling us that you danced with him yourself, are you?" Maria said.

"Indeed I did. I waltzed with him."

It is a rare young woman who is gratified that her sister danced with a duke when she herself did not. Neither Maria nor Henrietta were exceptions in this regard. "I only hope you will not give yourself airs, for I am sure you were of very little consequence to him," Maria said.

This stung Diana more than her sister could have known. And indeed had Maria known of her sister's tenderness for the Duke she would not have said it, for she was not wantonly cruel.

"I dare say you are right," Diana replied. Fortunately Mrs St Clair entered the room at that moment bearing an armful of flowers. For she, too, found it hard to be idle and consign every task to someone else. Flowers were a luxury they had not been able to afford in their previous home, and she delighted in picking and arranging such blooms now.

With Orchard House being so conveniently close to Bath, the St Clairs frequently welcomed visitors such as Mr and Mrs Harcourt. Jocasta Harcourt brought news of various acquaintances each time.

"Many people have left Bath and are gone to London or the country. We dined with the Granges last Friday and Leticia sends you all her best wishes. Only tell me of your stay at Eastleigh! For I know you have written to me of it, Catherine, but I am sure there is very much more to relate."

There was, but it was an ordeal for Diana to be reminded yet again. She listened as her mother gave select details, confining most of her remarks to the attributes of the house and grounds, rather than its inhabitants. Fortunately Mrs Harcourt was satisfied to learn of the furnishings of the various rooms, for this was a favourite subject of hers.

About three weeks after their return from Eastleigh, an elegant post chaise drew up bearing Charles and Susannah Lewis. Diana was delighted to greet the cousins, not knowing if or when Mr Lewis had left Eastleigh. The day was fine so the three of them took tea outside on the lawn.

"I left two days after you and your mother did," Charles informed her. "The party somewhat broke up after your departure."

"I am sorry," Diana said.

"Do not be. For I sensed I had outstayed my welcome as it was. With the Duke at any rate, if not his sister. His humour became markedly less genial towards me."

Diana asked how Lady Julia was. "I am sure she was very sad to see you go?"

There was a trace of embarrassment on Charles' face. "She is very well. In fact we have written to one another."

Diana was pleased to hear this and said so.

"I have told him he ought to propose to her. For he has barely spoken of anything or anyone else, and he has received no less than six letters from her," Susannah said. "But I did not come here to talk about my enamoured cousin's infatuations. Only tell me about the Duke. For when we last spoke of him, in Bath, you were certain that you had offended him. We were all sure that he must be a very arrogant and disagreeable person. And then to learn that he had invited you to his home! I have been so curious, but Charles has been little use in unravelling the mystery."

"There is no mystery. I believe that there was some confusion as to my identity which caused him to mistakenly suppose ill of me. But I have since discovered that he is a very gracious and courteous person. Indeed he is one of the most agreeable men I have ever met," Diana said. She gave herself away with this, for her voice trembled slightly.

The sharp-eyed Susannah was all attention. "Do not tell me - it cannot be - only it is, is it not? Your sentiments towards the Duke are so wholly altered as to be quite the reverse of what they were? And His Grace, was that also his true motive for inviting you to Eastleigh? O - do not mind Charles knowing of it all. For as he has assured us, he has no interest in gossip. We may take his discretion to be as sacred as the confessional seal, may we not, cousin?"

"With such a recommendation how could it not be?" her cousin replied.

"I only know that the Duke is supposedly engaged to Miss Wilde. Or soon to be so," Diana said.

Susannah was disappointed to learn this. "And I had fancied you had caught his eye! What say you, Charles?"

"Only that I am very surprised to hear it, since Julia never mentioned any arrangement. Rather the contrary. She despairs of her brother's eternal bachelorhood. And while I cannot claim I made a particular study of His Grace and to whom his affections might be directed, I saw no obvious signs of an understanding between Miss Wilde and him," Charles said.

"That makes it all the worse, then!" Diana blurted out. She checked herself but it was too late. Her friends' curiosity was aroused.

"What does?" Charles asked.

Diana was perturbed. "What was said - what was seen - by Mr Tanqueray. But I thought that you must know?" Her consternation grew as she saw blank bewilderment on Charles' face. "For Lady Julia was there, and we all heard."

"She said nothing to me concerning Mr Tanqueray. But what can he have seen that is such a matter of alarm?"

Susannah was even more intrigued. "You must tell us now,

Diana dear, or I shall be forced to write to the Duke himself to assuage my curiosity!"

Diana felt guilty for repeating the scandal but saw no way out, for her friends pressed her. "Mr Tanqueray claimed that he saw Miss Wilde enter the Duke of Eastleigh's bedchamber in the middle of the night. Then she departed - quite mysteriously and with no word to anyone - the next morning."

"Well that is absolutely extraordinary," Charles declared. "But whomever she may have spent the night with, it was not Eastleigh. For he spent the night in Chalmers' room."

Both Diana and Susannah were agog now. "In Mr Montague Chalmers room? But where was Mr Chalmers?" Diana asked.

Charles shrugged. "I cannot say. For all I know he was there as well, though I did not see him. But I rose early, and saw the Duke exiting Chalmers' bedroom and descending the stairs just as I opened my door to do likewise."

"What on earth can they all have been doing?" Susannah wondered. "Perhaps it is some novel game played by the peerage. Musical chairs, only with beds. We ought to find out, so that we might play it the next time my mother gives a party, Charles."

She was joking but Diana was too confused to feel light-hearted at that moment. Her thoughts were in turmoil. Had she badly misjudged the Duke? Charles's testimony might seem to dispel certain charges yet it left more questions than answers. "I no longer know what to think," she said, "if indeed I ever did. I know that Lady Julia was very distressed by it all."

Charles said he would write to her of it. "I will not mention that I heard anything from you. She will most likely assume Tanqueray became loose-lipped again. But there is a point I am curious on. How did you gain the impression that the pair of them - Eastleigh and Miss Wilde - were engaged?" he asked Diana.

"She told me so herself," Diana replied. "Or rather that there was an understanding between their families, that would soon result in an announcement."

"I am not sure whether that thickens or begins to clear the mystery," Susannah said. "What is she like, this woman? And how did she come to tell you this? For it seems that no one else knew of it, if Lady Julia did not."

The episode at Abbey Lake was still a very painful reminiscence for Diana. "She told me in the spirit of a sort of warning, though I am sure she thought she was being kind to me."

"A warning?" Susannah was bemused. "Tell us everything, for I see that it upsets you, and I fear you have been brooding on it. We may yet unravel it all and make better sense of this conundrum."

Diana revealed Miss Wilde's galling accusation. "She said that the Duke was embarrassed by my attitude towards him. She said - I can hardly bear to repeat it, for I was so ashamed - that I should 'stop trailing him like a lost lamb'."

Susannah gasped and burst out laughing. "How appalling! And so obviously untrue, for I know you well enough to know that you are not in the least capable of such behaviour. Do you not see that the woman was jealous of you, Diana, and sought to clear her own path? 'Kind' indeed!"

Charles agreed. "It is the most likely situation. The engagement was a mere fabrication. I also do not recall that he was sorry to see her go."

Diana felt that she had never been so glad to have such friends as Susannah and Charles Lewis. For weeks she had secretly fretted over Miss Wilde's remarks, but now a weight was lifted from her.

Though it was to some extent replaced by a new burden of remorse for having suspected the Duke of a wrongdoing of which he now seemed innocent.

It was a difficult letter that Charles Lewis wrote to Lady Julia. Of all the purported secret understandings and private betrothals there was one confirmed attachment: that between Charles and Julia. He had dared to ask for her hand before his departure and she had dared to accept. Though neither of them had yet dared to inform the Duke due to his darkened mood since the events at Eastleigh.

"My darling Julia, it is with some hesitation I write to you on a sensitive subject, but I hope it may bring you some reassurance to an issue that I fear may have been troubling you even though you have not spoken of it to me. Suffice it to say that although a certain lady was witnessed entering a certain bedchamber, the usual occupant of that bedchamber was not in residence that night. For I myself witnessed that person emerging from the room adjacent to mine on the following morning. I can shed no further light on the strange events of that night. But it was clearly not what people might have thought it was. And now onto other matters far dearer to my heart, which of course can only be my enduring love and adoration of your utter perfection…"

The rest of Mr Lewis's letter may be omitted here. Its recipient was equally relieved by both parts of his message. For where there has been more than a day without the post bringing confirmation of a lover's devotion, there must be severe torment, agony and doubt.

CHAPTER 26

It was now well into July and Diana had heard nothing more from anyone connected with Eastleigh. Susannah and Charles Lewis were gone to London and had invited her to accompany them, but Diana had declined. Orchard House was a sanctuary where she could escape her painful memories of the Duke. Charles' involvement with Lady Julia meant constant reminders of Eastleigh, and the fear that the Duke might reappear if he were in London.

Diana had exchanged several letters with Mary Hollis. She was delighted to learn that that another happy event was expected for the Hollises in a few months' time.

There was a letter from Lady Cavendish with an open invitation for Diana to visit her in Brighton or in London - *"for now Miss Havisham is restored to me, you may be entirely at your leisure should you stay with us."* She also wrote of a ball she planned to give in September at Grosvenor Square, and hoped that Diana and her sisters might attend.

"You cannot brood forever, Diana," Mrs St Clair said one morning as they sat in the salon. Diana had resumed her habit of reading the newspaper, only now she had the luxury of ordering whichever publications she wanted and having first read of them.

"I am not brooding, Mamma. I never think of him anymore."

Her mother knew that this was not the case. She wished that Diana had gone with her friends to London, believing the distraction would have been good for her. Maria and Henrietta were staying with friends again.

"Time will heal all, my dear," Mrs St Clair said.

The salon was positioned at the back of the house so they had not heard any vehicle arriving when Jenny rushed in bearing the news that a "very grand carriage" had just drawn up. "Four horses and a crest, and a driver all with livery!"

Diana and her mother looked at one another in alarm. They had not been expecting anyone and few of their friends travelled in anything near such grand style.

Mrs St Clair stood up, smoothing her hair and gown. "We will go and see who it is."

She and Diana went through the hall. Just as they came out of the front door, the carriage door opened. Amid the noise of bleating and wriggling, a tall figure emerged bearing two black and white-faced lambs.

It was the Duke of Eastleigh.

Diana did not know what to do. Conscious that her gown was creased and her hair not arranged as she would wish, she wondered why he should have come all this way.

The Duke approached them. "The lambs I promised you, now weaned and ready for their new home, if there is still room."

"It is most kind of you, Your Grace." Mrs St Clair's response was as composed as if he had presented her with flowers or merely his compliments. Diana marvelled at her mother's aplomb. Mrs St Clair called to Jenny. "Fetch Tom, if you would. You have had a comfortable journey, I trust?" she addressed the Duke again.

"A fine journey," he said, his eyes only on Diana. She was staring back, transfixed, at him.

"I hope you will excuse me while I instruct our cook to prepare some refreshments," Mrs St Clair said, though neither of the other two heard her or were aware of her leaving them.

The Duke looked taller and more commanding than Diana remembered. He was immaculately dressed, even holding the two sheep. She felt nervous yet unbearably happy to see him.

"It seems a very long time since I saw you," he said.

"It has been nine weeks," Diana replied.

"It has been nearer ten."

They were silent again, interrupted only by the arrival of Tom, to whom the Duke gladly offloaded the lambs. When the shepherd boy had gone the Duke spoke again. "You look well. Have you been well?"

"I have, Your Grace. I hope the same is so for you?"

"It is not," the Duke told her. "Will you walk with me?"

Diana led him through the orchard, towards the river, a tributary of the Avon, that wound its way past the end of the trees. When they reached it they stopped, unable to proceed further. The Duke turned to Diana.

"I know I am probably a fool for even speaking, and you doubtless consider me far too old, but I believe I have never been so happy as when you graced my home at Eastleigh. I would that you were there always."

"I do not consider you old, Your Grace."

The Duke extended his hands, and Diana took them. "Will you allow me to hope that there may one day come a time when you might feel enough affection for me to become my wife?" he asked.

Diana only knew that her entire being felt suffused by a kind of golden light. Struggling to keep her voice steady, she said: "I cannot allow you to hope that, my lord."

Alarm and disappointment flared in his eyes, until she continued.

"For I do so already. If it is not presumptuous of me?"

Joy broke across his grave features. He laughed. "It is not presumptuous. It is something I have longed for. For I love you. I think I have done so from the first moment I saw you. Though I had not the sense to realise it at first." He grew serious again. "Will you be with me always? Be my wife? I do not want to rush you, for I am conscious of your years. Our engagement can be as long as you wish."

"Then I wish it to be a very short one."

Joy replaced his solemnity once more. He moved his hands to her face, cupping it, and brought his lips down upon hers. They were as warm and firm as Diana remembered. As she had longed for. The embrace deepened and his arms went around her, and she instinctively wound hers around him, pulling him closer.

He broke off and looked at her, his eyes darkened. "Diana." It was the first time he had spoken her name.

"My lord."

"My name is James," he told her.

"James," she breathed, reaching up to him again and this time instigating the kiss. As she broke off, she finally spoke the words he had been desperate to hear. "I love you, James."

Urgently his mouth came down on hers again, desire flaring in him. His hands moved over her, feeling the slender curves that would soon be his. He adored how she arched into him when he cupped her rear and pressed him against him. The soft moan that caught in her throat when he daringly moved a hand across her breast. He knew he would end up taking her then and there if he did not exert more self-control, and he wanted to wait until the proper time. She was a maiden, and he owed her that.

Summoning all his strength he separated from her again, loving the flush on her face and her half closed eyes.

"I love you," he said again. "But we had better continue to walk."

He linked his arm through hers as they walked along the river bank.

"Why did you leave me so suddenly?" the Duke asked.

"I had thought you engaged to Miss Wilde."

There was a bitter note in his laugh. "I was never engaged to that woman."

"I am sorry. I was confused… by circumstances," Diana said.

"I think I know what those circumstances were. I would like to explain them to you."

Diana protested. "There is no need, my lord. It all seems very long ago, and no longer matters."

"Nonetheless, I wish to do so. And if I may command anything of you, as your lord, it is that you will call me by my name," the Duke said.

"James."

"That is better. Now, to that fateful night. I have heard what Mr Tanqueray said, and I regret to say that he did not imagine what he saw. I have also heard what Mr Lewis bears witness to, but I am afraid I cannot claim to have spent the entire night in that room either. In short, I went to my bed quite alone. I awoke before dawn to discover that a person had… sleepwalked into my chamber. I left at once, and Mr Chalmers suggested exchanging places."

"Sleepwalked?" As she spoke, Diana realised the truth of this courteous lie as the situation became clear. She felt a wave of sympathy for Miss Wilde. What a devious thing to have done, to have entered a man's bedroom in the hope of entrapping him. And how mortified she must have been the next morning!

"In retrospect it was not a chivalrous act to have swapped with Mr Chalmers," the Duke continued. "But to have done anything else would likely have meant I could never be here with you."

"Then I am very glad you did what you did," Diana said. "And Mr Chalmers too."

The Duke agreed. "He has my eternal thanks. But I do not wish to talk of Monty at this moment. Tell me when you first knew you loved me."

"When I first knew or when I first did?"

"Both," he demanded.

"I first realised at the picnic, when your sister asked me if I had an understanding with Charles Lewis. I thought about it and realised he did not arouse the same feelings in me as you did. And when I first loved you? I think from the very first time you scowled at me in Bath, for I could never get you out of my mind after that time," Diana told him.

"Nor I you. How much time we have wasted."

They had reached the foot of the field where the sheep grazed. They watched the lambs gambolling about. "I would ask you a question," Diana said.

"You may ask me anything you like, since I am now to be your husband."

"Were I to have sleepwalked to your bedchamber, would you have escaped and spent the night elsewhere?"

"I would have carried you to my bed myself and locked us both in there. Which I thoroughly intend to do once I get you back to Eastleigh." Then he recalled her inexperience. "You understand that there are certain intimacies that take place between a husband and wife? You may decide you are not ready for that, and I can be patient if so."

Diana blushed, for she was not entirely ignorant of such matters. She had an image of how the Duke might be on their wedding night, and it was not unwelcome. "I do understand, my lord."

They continued to walk along together, each entirely happy to be with the other.

"How did you decide to come today?" Diana said.

"I have wanted to come and see you ever since you left, but I did not dare. When you left I thought you must revile me, for what you thought I had done. I wanted to explain myself but thought it futile. For I believed you to be in love with Charles Lewis," the Duke said.

"He is a good friend, but I have never been in love with him. I am sorry if anything in my conduct led you to believe so,"

Diana said.

"It was nothing in your conduct. I had been informed that you had an understanding with him. By the same person who told you that I was engaged to her, I warrant?" Diana nodded and the Duke continued. "I regret that I was foolish enough to believe it. But even if you did not want him, I doubted that you might ever want me. And then there was the obstacle of your age. It did not help that from every corner I heard the ridicule over the Ponsonby marriage."

She laughed at this. "I am hardly a Mrs Ponsonby, James. For I am not in need of any fortune you might have. I come freely. And although I have never met the unfortunate Mr Ponsonby, I am reliably informed that he is some twenty years older than you and resembles a haddock."

"I do not resemble a haddock?"

She reached up for his face, daring to trace her fingers over his features for the first time. "You are everything I could ever want."

Once again the Duke had the strange sensation that this girl, half his years, unworldly and without title, was entirely his equal. He was not sure whether she kissed him or he kissed her, but within a few moments of losing himself in her again, it did not seem to matter.

Afterwards the Duke insisted that he speak formally with her mother. "For she may yet refuse her consent."

Diana knew that her mother would not refuse. Mrs St Clair might prefer that they waited a year or so, but she would not force a delay on them.

The Duke held his interview with Mrs St Clair while Diana waited in the salon. He returned, to tell her that her mother wished to speak with her.

There was as much concern as joy on Mrs St Clair's face when her daughter entered. "Are you very sure, my dear? For it is not a decision that can ever easily be unmade."

"I cannot be without him, Mamma. I only want to be with him."

It echoed what Mrs St Clair had once said, many years ago, to a kind friend concerned about her acceptance of Rainault's proposal. *"Be very sure, Catherine, for there is little fortune there, and you have none."* But Catherine Harborough had known her own mind then as her daughter did now.

"Nor do I suppose you can be persuaded to the caution of a long engagement?" she asked.

"Not unless you very desperately wish it, Mamma."

"My only wish is that you are happy, both of you, for many years. You are eighteen now, which is young, but I was only nineteen when I married your father. And I have never regretted that. Come, then. You have my happy consent, though I am sure I will miss you terribly, my dear."

CHAPTER 27

Few could remember ever seeing a bride as fair as the youngest St Clair girl when she married the Duke of Eastleigh. The guests were not many, for both bride and groom wished for a small, private affair.

It was not the flowers entwined in her hair, or the white silk and net gown wrought with silver lilies, or even the Beresford diamonds that crowned her golden head in a glittering tiara that gave her such radiance.

It was the happiness on her face as she gazed at James Beresford, now her husband, as they walked from the altar together.

No wonder Eastleigh had finally got hooked, Montague Chalmers considered, standing by his friend in church. The girl was beyond compare. Too young to be a duchess, surely. Yet she had more poise than a dozen women Monty could think of with ten or more years on her.

Diana was attended by her sisters. Being older and unmarried themselves, this might have been an uncomfortable situation. But Henrietta had finally secured a proposal from a viscount, and Maria was considering two different offers, both from very eligible and wealthy gentlemen with no designs on her fortune. It was thus a very happy state of affairs for the St Clair family.

Diana was glad to see everyone and grateful for their best wishes, but longed for it all to be over so she could be with her new husband. She had not seen the Duke for some weeks before the wedding. It had been an anxious time for her. She had frequently feared that something might go wrong. That he might change his mind, or some other disaster might befall.

She felt as much relief as happiness to finally be reunited with him, unknowing that the Duke had suffered exactly the same turmoil. Even more severely than his bride had, if truth be told.

"We ought to have eloped," he murmured in her ear. "For I do not know how I can endure a banquet before being alone with you. It has been too long. I am even tempted to take a carriage and drive off with you now."

The feast was a sight to behold. The kitchens of Eastleigh had covered themselves in glory with the variety and splendour of the dishes served. Since it was September and still warm, there were ices scattered with crystallised petals of rose and violet. Peaches and apricots from the greenhouses at Eastleigh were piled high on crystal platters, with bunches of frosted grapes cascading down. A snow-white wedding cake adorned with blossoms graced the centre of the table.

Diana, despite the magnificence of it all, could barely eat a morsel. Fortunately her guests had ready appetites for the delicacies.

There were tears as Mrs St Clair and her elder daughters departed. They had been invited to stay at Eastleigh as the journey back to Bath would be too far to complete before nightfall. But Mrs St Clair thought it best for the newlyweds to be free of guests and the duties of host. With this in mind she had arranged a night's lodging elsewhere.

Finally alone, the Duke led Diana to his bedchamber. It was by now late evening for a couple of less considerate guests had lingered.

She stood there in her finery, the diamonds glittering in her hair. Her beauty moved him: he could hardly believe she was his. Yet below her eyes he saw the smudges of tiredness and that she was paler than usual.

He should let her rest, he thought. He went to her and put

his arms around her, holding her against him. "My love."

She turned up her face towards him and he kissed her gently. It was hard to restrain himself from deepening the embrace but he did not want to alarm or exhaust her. They had all the time in the world. There was no need for everything tonight.

She was looking expectantly at him. "James?"

"You should sleep, my darling. We have endless days and nights ahead of us." Was it relief or regret he saw in her eyes? He could not say. The scent of her and the warmth of her consumed him. "Only let me help you disrobe, rather than summon the maid."

He lifted the tiara from her head and placed it onto a table. Her gown was trickier, with its tiny hooks, but the Duke's hands were deft. He let it slip to the floor and she stood there in her chemise. The fabric was so fine it seemed filmy and he could not resist gently tracing the outline of her waist and hips with his hands, feeling her shiver and move towards him as he did so.

Her eyes were on him all the time, trusting, desiring. She raised her hands and he first thought she meant to push him away. Instead her fingers went to loosen the cravat at his neck, reaching below to undo the buttons of his collar.

He helped her here, for the starch made them difficult and he felt how her hands trembled. Easing out of his jacket, his neck and the upper part of his chest now exposed to her, he stiffened as her fingers traced his skin. She was hesitant but wanted to touch him.

The Duke was on fire for her, even at this light contact. He took a deep breath and exhaled, steadying himself. He had every intention of civilised behaviour but suspected it was going to stretch the limits of his control. He longed to have her naked before him but feared to rush her, so removed his own shirt first.

His bride was hesitant at first, viewing the broad expanse of his chest and the muscles of his arms. The Duke was disciplined about physical activity, fencing regularly at a club in London. There was a scar, too, from a duel he had fought and won many years ago.

Diana ran her finger over this now and looked at it questioningly. "It is an old wound, my lord?"

"Long healed. A friend of mine's wife was impugned, and since he was wounded in battle I stood for him," the Duke told her.

"I hope I shall never be the reason for you to risk yourself. For I could not bear to see you hurt."

"If you had been the one impugned, my opponent would not have escaped with his life," was her husband's reply. "But are you not too fatigued for this, my love? We may simply lie together."

She was resolute. "I wish to be your wife. From now. I do not want to wait any longer."

He kissed her then, feeling their mutual dissolution in one another. He hoped she understood what was meant by her words. She had indicated that she did but she may have only had the vaguest of ideas. The situation was novel to the Duke of Eastleigh as well. His past mistresses had been women of the world for want of a better term: either married or widowed, or at least well accustomed to relations between men and women.

He had never taken a maiden before. It was generally considered a blackguardly and ignoble act. Even though it was legal and sanctified to do so with his own wife he felt a qualm of conscience about her innocence.

He unlaced her chemise and let it fall, drawing in his breath as he beheld the beauty of her slim form. Embracing her again he picked her up and carried her to the bed, laying her down and then removing the rest of his clothes. He held his body away from her, not wanting to scare her, while he caressed her in secret and formerly forbidden places until she was panting and reaching for him.

"I do not want to cause you pain, Diana. But you understand that there may be discomfort?"

She did. "Only the first time, I believe."

He lay over her now and she felt the weight of him, his masculinity hard against her thigh. Firmly but with gentleness he parted her own thighs, and exerting more control than he had thought possible, made her his with infinite care and tenderness. She did cry out and the sound of it wrenched him as much as it inflamed him.

He started to withdraw but she clung to him whispering: "No, please stay with me. It is alright, it grows easier."

So he waited, overcome with love and desire for her. And when she was able to resume he took it as slowly as he could, all the while caressing her where he knew it would distract her from any discomfort.

To his amazement and delight she soon met his passion with hers and cried out and moved against him in quite a different manner. This did not always happen with women, or not so easily, and he was glad for Diana and for himself that she was so responsive.

There were other precautions the Duke had intended to take, not wanting to risk certain outcomes so soon in their marriage. But he was so engulfed by love and desire that he failed to hold back.

Diana felt dizzy as she lay in her husband's arms. The heat still throbbed throughout her body but it was a glowing, happy warmth. She was profoundly grateful to Mary Hollis for her advice. Diana had stayed with the Hollises in London while buying items for her trousseau, and Mary had educated her with quite candid details. She saw no sense in leaving another woman in ignorance, for a little knowledge might make the wedding night pleasanter for both bride and groom.

While Mrs St Clair had shared some information, it was Mary's frankness that had better prepared Diana for this event. Even though she had found some of the details shocking at the time.

Now she felt utterly content. She was his and she thought, or hoped, that she had not disappointed him. He lay upon her, his breathing still heavy, his skin damp with perspiration. She feared he was exhausted. "You are well, my lord?"

He eased off her and looked down at her, laughing softly at the concern he saw in her eyes. "I am more than well, my darling. It is you of whom I should be asking that question."

"I am more well than I have ever been," Diana replied. "Only never leave me."

He laughed again at that and kissed her. "I will never leave you." His hand moved down to cup and caress her breast, and Diana felt her skin tingle and tauten at the sensation. "You are more beautiful than I could ever have imagined."

Diana recalled other advice that Mary had given her about recovery on the following day. She had advised rest and bathing, and no other strenuous activities until a woman felt quite recovered.

For now Diana only wanted to sleep. She felt a great weariness suffuse her. Her one confusion was that an adjoining chamber had been prepared for her at Eastleigh and she was not sure if she was supposed to return to it. The Duke saw the conflict in her expression as he gazed at her and asked her what was wrong.

"I only wondered if you would prefer me to return to the other room until morning," she said.

Her husband was confounded for a moment, then realised her inexperience. "I can safely say that I would not prefer it," he told her. "I want you here with me. And not just tonight, but always. Unless you want to sleep separately?"

"Not at all. I wasn't sure... what married people did," Diana said. Her parents had shared a room and so had the Hollises in London. But such a to-do had been made about redecorating the "Duchess's chamber" that she wasn't entirely sure of its purpose or her role in occupying it.

"What other married people do is up to them. I dare say there may be times when you are unwell, or so annoyed with me that you prefer to stay there with the key on your side."

He was joking but she took him seriously. "I could never be annoyed with you."

"I will hold you to that, in future, when we squabble over my gambling debts or the price of your gowns."

Now they both laughed, for she realised that he was teasing her. He had so frequently seemed a grave, authoritative figure - all the more so when he stood so tall and dignified next to her in church - that his lighter side delighted her.

It was difficult to become accustomed to the idea that she was now a duchess. For the Duke's rank had never been his attraction for her. It had been his solitariness, a remote quality, that had set him apart from the crowd. Something that had evoked her sympathy, as young and lowly as she was compared to him. It had made her want to be with him for his sake. Even as his masculine good looks and physique had aroused more womanly desires in her.

And now those desires could be expressed and mutually satisfied. "You are not displeased with me, are you, my lord? For how I was, some moments earlier." She felt shy to phrase it for what it was.

"Once again it is I who should be asking you that. I am more than pleased, my darling. I am overjoyed by you and only desire you even more after our lovemaking. But now we must both sleep and recover our strength."

He held her, and safe in his embrace and the knowledge he would not leave her, she closed her eyes and let oblivion overtake her.

CHAPTER 28

One year later

The following June it was not only the Cotswold Longhorn ewes who bore twins. The Duke of Eastleigh, when finally allowed to enter his own bedchamber, discovered not one but two arrivals in the cradle beside the bed.

His attention was more on his wife. To his huge relief although she looked exhausted she seemed otherwise happy. She smiled at him as he entered. It had been a difficult birth and the Duke had spent a night of agony fearing he would lose both Diana and their unborn child.

"All is well, Your Grace," the attending physician told him. "Her Grace will need extensive rest I but I anticipate that she will make a full recovery."

The doctor departed with the midwife, leaving the Duke alone with his duchess.

"My darling, forgive me for being the reason for this," he said, taking her hands in his and kissing her forehead. He indicated the cradle. "Did you know?"

"I did not, nor I think did the doctor. But I suspect the midwife knew. Likely she did not reveal it in case of causing me anxiety," Diana said.

The Duke looked over again at his heirs, one of which was slightly larger than the other. "One of each?" he asked.

"Your daughter came just ten minutes after your son. We will need to find names for them."

"St Clair James Beresford," the Duke suggested, regarding the larger infant.

"A very fine name. I am sure she will be delighted by it," his wife replied.

Puzzled for a moment, the Duke realised his error. "This

one is the girl?"

"It is indeed."

He chuckled. "Her brother had better watch his step. How about Catherine, after your mother?"

"You wouldn't prefer your mother's name?" Diana asked. "I have only heard her spoken of as Fanny, but that was surely a nickname? She was Frances, perhaps, or Francesca?"

The Duke grimaced. "I doubt you will like it. My grandfather was a scholar of the Classics and something of an eccentric. She was christened Theophane. I also had an Uncle Agamemnon and an Aunt Clytemnestra, both now deceased. So you may consider my own mother got off lightly."

His wife, despite her fatigue, was laughing. "But that is perfect!"

"I'm glad you find it amusing."

"No, you don't understand. There's the myth of Theophane. I only know of it because it was noted as a curiosity in a journal on sheep husbandry that Lord Cavendish lent me. Theophane was a mythical maiden whom one of the gods turned into a sheep."

"A sheep?" The Duke looked again at his daughter. "A Welsh Hill or a Cotswold Longhorn? Catherine Theophane it is, then."

The Lady Catherine Theophane Beresford accepted her name with a loud wail. "You had better give her to me," Diana said.

"Should we not call the nurse?"

"Let me try first," Diana urged.

Having no experience at all with babies, the Duke was initially in some consternation as to how to pick the child up. He finally managed to scoop her into his hands and pass her to his wife. In Diana's arms the wails rapidly subsided as she loosened the neck of her gown and held the infant to her breast. This had been another lesson from Mary Hollis, who had refused a wet nurse for her own children. Diana was determined to try likewise.

Encouraged, the Duke picked up his small son and regarded him. "He has very little hair," he observed. The Lord St Clair James Beresford, who was not yet aware that he was also the Most Honble. The Marquess of Dalebury began wailing at this.

"You had better call the nurse, for I am not sure that my capabilities yet reach to two," Diana said.

Gratefully her husband did so. Even tired, with her hair tousled and an infant clasped to her, he thought she had never looked more alluring. During his sleepless hours the previous night he had been so desperately worried for her and so guilty for his role in her pain, that he had vowed never again to risk putting her in the same situation. Even if it meant years of enforced celibacy.

Now, as the nurse took the baby from him, the Duke regarded his wife and doubted it was a vow he would be able to keep for very long.

It had been a wonderful year. The Duke and his new duchess had found themselves matched in many more ways than they had originally realised.

Diana had first thought that she would often be expected to remain at Eastleigh while her husband had business to attend to elsewhere. She soon found that this was not the case. The Duke wanted her with him everywhere.

The thought of managing a household as large as Eastleigh had initially overwhelmed her as well. But seeing how efficiently it had run for many years without a mistress, she had wisely left as much as possible in the hands of the capable housekeeper and other staff.

Friends visited Eastleigh and they Duke and Duchess paid visits in their turn. They had enjoyed a happy couple of weeks at Cavendish House, though Lady Cavendish had not withheld her own opinion of their marriage.

"I suppose I am to congratulate you, Eastleigh, but as you must be aware I thoroughly disapprove," she announced on greeting them. "What kind of a Bluebeard are you, to lock up this young woman in that mausoleum of a house of yours?"

The accusation had been so outrageous that Diana could not help laughing. Her husband, well used to Honoria Cavendish's outspokenness, also smiled.

Later Lady Cavendish had given Diana a considerably less unfavourable view of their union. She had invited Diana to her room, where she had presented her with a beautiful sapphire and pearl brooch as a wedding gift. "I dare say Eastleigh won't make the worst of husbands. He is not given to vices, he has the affection of his friends and he has some degree of intelligence," she said. There was a soft twinkle in her eye as she looked at Diana, adjusting the brooch on her gown. "And perhaps what is most important above all, I do not think I have ever seen a man so in love with anyone."

For the Duke, the past year had been a revelation. He no longer had any wish to be solitary. There had been difficult moments, such as when some man had been talking to Diana, making no secret that he found her alluring. The Duke had felt such a surge of jealousy that for a moment his old fury was back.

Then she had turned to him, and he saw the plea in her eyes. She had murmured: "I am so tired, James, can we leave soon?" and he had realised her smiling at the other man was nothing but courtesy. It was he, her husband, whom she sought. Whom she turned to.

After that he had been able to look upon her conversing

with others with more equanimity. She was young and beautiful and it was natural that she had many admirers. But over time he had been increasingly reassured by her devotion to him and him alone.

Now of course he must share that devotion with not one but two offspring. The Duke looked again at the two small bundles, marvelling at how two new people could suddenly have appeared in the world.

"Your mother should arrive this evening. I have ordered the rose room to be prepared for her, unless you think she would prefer another?" he asked.

Mrs St Clair had planned to arrive well in time for the birth but the twins had made their appearance two weeks early. This was not uncommon, so the midwife had told Diana.

"The rose room will be perfect." Diana exchanged the babies with the nurse, now offering her son his first feed. "And Julia and Charles will still come at the start of August?" The Duke had finally permitted his sister to accept Charles Lewis's proposal, a softening of opinion that his wife had played no small part in. They had married that May.

"Yes. With Miss Lewis," the Duke said.

Diana's sisters were both away. Henrietta and her viscount were on a wedding tour in the Lake District, with Maria accompanying them. Maria had still not decided on a suitor though she did not want for offers.

The Duke lingered while Diana nursed until the midwife ordered him out of the room so his wife could rest. The midwife's duty to her patient superseded any deference to a husband, be he a duke or even the Prince Regent, as she informed Diana.

Oblivion came quickly, for Diana was exhausted throughout every fibre of her being.

The days and weeks passed peacefully. The twins thrived, with the assistance of a wet nurse as Diana found two babies harder to manage than she had thought. The Duke, who had assumed the children would largely be kept out of sight in the nursery until they were older, found himself taking an active interest in them.

The weather remained warm throughout August, and the Duke and Diana sat among the late blooms in the rose garden. "I have been wondering if any changes should be made to this garden. New bushes, perhaps, in honour of the twins?"

Diana liked the idea. "But do not change things too much. For this place is very dear to me, and I love it just as it is."

The Duke looked at her in surprise. "I had not known you were so fond of it."

Even as a married woman of more than a year and the mother of two children, Diana could still blush. "You do not remember, James?"

Her husband remembered and smiled. "It is where I first kissed you, is it not? A presumption which at the time I greatly castigated myself for."

"I do not castigate you, now or then. For though I thought it must be very wrong, believing you betrothed to another, I cannot say I resented it in the slightest. You may now call me a wanton if you like."

She was teasing him, a frequent habit to lighten his moods when he grew grave. But he was not grave at that moment. His lips came down upon hers and his body reacted as powerfully as it had done that first time. Weeks of abstinence while his wife recovered from the birth had done nothing to quell his ardour. Quite the reverse.

"So long as you are wanton with me and no other, I thoroughly approve of it," he murmured as he embraced her neck, his hands running over the body that had recently been forbidden to him.

"I am very glad that you approve it. For the prescribed time is up, and you may count your restful nights at an end."

He sat up. "You mean we may - ?"

"Exactly so. Tonight, if you wish," Diana said.

The Duke decided there were far too many hours until evening. Figuring they were shielded well enough by the tall yew hedges, he scooped his wife up and laid her on the soft grass between the rose beds.

Diana protested, laughing. But any resistance soon dissolved as his hands moved to where they had been longing to go, and his mouth covered hers again.

Surrounded by the bower of roses, their fragrance filling the air, the Duke showed his Duchess just how much he approved of her. How much he loved and desired her, and always would.

About Noël Cades

Noël Cades is a British writer who currently lives in Sydney, Australia. A fan of romance, particularly historic, some of Noël's favourite authors include Jilly Cooper, Georgette Heyer, Elizabeth Rolls, Anne Mather, Charlotte Lamb, Sara Seale, Victoria Holt and (of course!) Jane Austen.

Noël is always delighted to hear from other fans, readers and writers of romance.

You can contact Noël at noelcades@gmail.com

Noël's website is at **www.noelcades.com**

Visit Noël's blog to sign up for exclusive news and the chance to receive new free book giveaways.

More hot, forbidden romances by Noël Cades available in paperback:

Falling From Grace
Gabriel entered the priesthood after a betrayal left him bitter. But when he meets troubled, beautiful Leonie, he wonders if he made the right choice.

His Model Student
When Sera's new art teacher mistakes her for a model and demands that she strip naked, sparks start to fly. Will Mr Marek be able to keep his student at arm's length after seeing everything she has to offer?

Tempting Her Teacher
Catholic school teacher Carl Spencer faces a crisis of faith when he falls for his student Juliet, how can he resist the temptation to be with her? But while he struggles to resist his growing attraction, she's starting to realise that it's become more than just a game for her.

Summer's Edge
When sports coach Stewart Walker finds out the girl he kissed is a student at his school he's furious and determined to keep away. But 18-year-old Alice has fallen hard and won't give up.

Man of the Match
Broken-hearted student Cara has no idea that the handsome stranger who seduced her on holiday is England cricket captain Matt Curran. Shocking twists and sexy action in the glamorous world of international cricket.

Excerpts from The Substitute Bride by Noël Cades:

"But you'll do it? Oh please, Lily, I'll die if I have to go through with it. You are my last, my only hope."

Lily Cosgrove looked at the distraught, tear-stained face of her cousin Betsy. She was pale in the candle-light, her eyes dark hollows from sleepless nights. Outside the wind howled and a tree rattled against the window panes.

It was a wild night for a wedding.

But wilder still was Betsy's plan. For Lily to swap places with her, and marry the unknown man who was coming that night to save her family's honour. He had never met either of them: how was he to know if a substitute Elizabeth Cosgrove stood before him at the altar?

Lily wanted to help her cousin but she was conflicted.

"What if we were discovered? Would it even be a valid marriage?"

"I am sure it would. Oh, Lily, if I am forced to marry him it means I can never, ever be with Tom. I simply couldn't bear that!"

No thought was given to Lily's own fate, but then she had never enjoyed the same expectations as Betsy. Orphaned and penniless, her uncle had reluctantly taken her into his household, avoiding spending a farthing more on his niece than required.

Lily didn't care if Sir Robert was cold and indifferent to her, for she loved Betsy and was grateful for a home. She reminded herself that he was her father's only brother and had done his duty by her.

So the two girls grew up together, Lily a year younger than Betsy. They had been happy enough. But then Betsy had her first Season - there were no such plans to waste money debuting Lily in Society - and met the Honourable Tom Farrington.

She had allowed herself to be seduced by him, and worse, got caught in flagrante delicto. The less-than-honourable Tom had bolted to the continent at the first opportunity, leaving Betsy bereft.

Although it soon became apparent that there wasn't going to be the complication of a child, Betsy was nonetheless ruined and her family's name tainted with her.

Darkness descended on the household. Invitations were cancelled. Weeks followed of furious silence from Sir Robert and hand-wringing and recrimination from Lady Maud. She even managed to cast blame on her niece despite Lily not even being there. Not being out in Society, Lily had never even met the infamous Tom Farrington. But her aunt was too distraught to acknowledge this. How could her beloved daughter have had this happen to her? Others must surely be at fault!

The servants, well aware of everything that had gone on, remained tight-lipped but they cast one another glances and Lily knew they must gossip about the scandal behind closed doors.

Poor Betsy. One foolish mistake and she carried all the burden of censure and condemnation. And despite Tom running out on her she still adored him. She was still convinced he would come for her, though Lily feared this was very unlikely.

Then a surprise offer of help arrived. Tom's cousin, the Marquess of Westford, had written to Betsy's father proposing marriage to save her family's honour. A very private man who rarely left his country estate, he had expressed shame and embarrassment at his young relative's actions and wished to make good the situation.

Sir Robert was only too glad to take the Marquess up on his offer. The marriage would be held in the chapel of his own home. He and his wife were away at the time the correspondence took place. Lady Maud was taking a "rest cure", unable to bear the proximity of neighbours and staff who knew all about their dishonour.

"We will remain at Buxton due to my wife's condition. It is desirable that this event takes place with the least delay," Sir Robert wrote.

He preferred to distance himself from the entire affair and his daughter's disgrace. If in time her reputation were redeemed in the eyes of society, he might again acknowledge her.

So Betsy would get married alone. The local curate would give her away. There would be no wedding gown, no trousseau. It was purely an arrangement.

Lily smoothed the worn muslin of her own gown over her lap. It was a cast off of Betsy's, she was rarely given new clothes of her own. Her uncle considered that she didn't need them as she wasn't out in society. Now she almost certainly never would be.

The candles flickered. The evening drew on. Tonight the Marquess would come for his bride.

"They say he's a confirmed bachelor, he must be ancient, Lily! And I know Tom means to return. He loves me Lily, I am certain! This horrid cousin and his disapproval are the very reason we had to keep our love secret, and why he had to flee abroad."

As inexperienced as Lily was, she doubted this. But she did not want to upset Betsy further.

Betsy's accusations against the Marquess hardly encouraged Lily to agree to take her place, but she knew her own fortunes were very different to her cousin's. Lily had no money for a dowry, so with his duty done, her uncle planned to send her to live as the companion of a distant relation. This lady, an elderly dowager of irascible temper, lived in the remote Highlands far away from society. A bleak and gruelling future lay ahead..

Maybe to be the mistress of a household, any household, was better?

But it was not this consideration that made Lily finally agree to her cousin's desperate plan. It was out of genuine concern for Betsy, and the faintest hope that Tom might yet return for her. Since there was no prospect of love in Lily's own life, it was surely but a slight sacrifice for her to be confined by matrimonial bonds?

Still, she wavered. What if this was the best outcome for Betsy? Even if this Marquess were elderly, he was a rich and noble man and Betsy would want for nothing. She would regain her place in society and perhaps even bear children if the Marquess were not quite so decrepit as feared.

"Very well."

As she spoke the words, she had the strangest sensation that the walls were at once closing in and crumbling down around her.

"Oh Lily!" Betsy was in raptures amid a fresh outburst of tears. Her relief, that saw her breaking down even more than before, vindicated Lily's decision. Marrying this man was almost a matter of indifference to her, but to Betsy it was a prison sentence.

Now all she had to do was go through with it. Approach the altar, speak her vows, and leave for she knew not where.

* * *

Lily was exhausted. All she wanted to do was get beneath the eiderdown and sleep. She opened her trunk, finding some small comfort in the familiar items inside.

There was a knock on the door and the landlady - for most of the other servants were in bed by this late hour - entered with a tray and set it down on the small table by the chair.

"Here you are, my lady. Is there anything else you need?"

There wasn't so Lily thanked her.

The tavern woman was curious about this nervous looking girl, arriving with such a rich and titled husband. She had first thought the worst but glancing at Lily's hand, saw the ring there.

"Newly married, are you?" The girl was so young and tense, she didn't have the assurance of a long married woman.

"Yes." Lily couldn't bring herself to say "earlier tonight". It seemed indecent, as though it still lacked propriety for her to be sharing a room with a man. "Recently."

"My belated congratulations, my lady." She saw a shadow pass over Lily's face and interpreted it as the typical bedroom fears of a new bride. It took a while to get used to these things, after all. As like as not the man downstairs was a boorish beast when it came to taking his rights. Titled or not - and the landlady had entertained both in her time, make no mistake about that - they were all the same. They needed a firm hand, but what mere woman's strength could counter a man's lusty force?

The landlady had given her own daughter some choice advice on her nuptials, as well as the recipe for a brew that would cool the ardour, quell the loins and hasten sleep. But it was not her place to suggest any such thing to this girl. A marchioness she must be, fancy that! Staying in her own humble inn.

Wanting to do at least something for her the stout tavern woman lifted another log onto the fire and gave it a good poke, sending a shower of sparks up the chimney. The young bride wouldn't freeze to death at least.

"Good night then, and anything you need, you let me know," she said, taking her leave.

Lily was alone once more.

On the tray lay a dish of stew with a rich gravy, a hunk of bread and a tankard of weak ale. It smelled appetising and she should have felt hungry but something constricted her throat. She could barely manage a morsel.

Oh Betsy, Betsy, what have we done? How can I bear this alone?

She drew out of the trunk a nightgown made of fine lawn. It was Betsy's, her cousin must have slipped it in there as a gift. The filminess of the fabric was like silk compared to Lily's own plainer cotton one. Quickly she undressed before the fire and put it on, folding away her muslin dress as best she could. She loosened and removed her own stays.

It was lovely to have her own fire, even in these circumstances. Sir Robert never allowed them in bedrooms and in winter there was frequently ice on the inside of Lily's window pane.

Despite her exhaustion she was too wound up to sleep so she took a book of verse she had packed, sat in the small chair, and started reading.

She was lost in the poetry when there was a knock at the door. Startled, she said "come in!" and then rose to her feet in shock as the Marquess entered. Her husband.

Will the Marquess demand his rights? Will he discover that Lily is not the fallen woman he believes her to be? Find out what happens in Lily's wedding night in The Substitute Bride, a Regency Romance by Noël Cades.